SISTERS' GARDEN
OF SECRETS

A Novel by

Pearl Preston

SISTERS' GARDEN OF SECRETS
by Pearl Preston

Copyright © 2020 Pearl Preston

Published by
Maker's Mark Press

Cover and Interior Design by Nick Zelinger

ISBN: 978-0-9980689-2-3 (print)
ISBN: 978-0-9980689-3-0 (eBook)
Library of Congress Cataloging in Publication Data

First Edition

Printed in the United States of America

To my beautiful sister, and all sisters everywhere who are bonded together by a lifetime of secrets, laughter, and tears.

CHAPTER ONE

"There's a special kind of freedom sisters enjoy. Freedom to share innermost thoughts, to ask a favor, to show their true feelings. The freedom to simply be themselves."

Monet would be jealous of this garden, Isabella thought, enjoying a brilliant floral view from her kitchen window.

From her vantage point at the kitchen table, she had a panoramic view of her very own English flower garden—each delicate petal an expression of her sister's warmth and wholehearted love. "I am planting this garden for you, Isabella," her older sister Johanna had told her years ago, "as another way to show how much I love you."

"And you've done just that," Isabella whispered, excited that her sister would be visiting her within the hour. No one was closer to her than Johanna. The bond that was forged between them from childhood abuse, to later, breaking free to succeed as adults, was now stronger than cooled molten steel.

Memories drifted in, just as they always did during a day, as if riding on windblown clouds. Isabella placed her coffee cup down, rose from the chair, and walked outside to enjoy the afternoon sun. It always seemed like summer took an eternity to arrive, but when it did—the English garden bloomed once again and so did Isabella's favorite pastime—gathering a handful of roses.

"We've shared so many secrets," Isabella smiled, thinking of Johanna as she snipped a few Lady of Shalott roses. Inhaling the light tea scent of the bronze blossoms, she closed her eyes, sighed, and like a rushing tide, the memories surged.

The year had been 1945. She'd been only four years old at the time and Johanna was six. They'd been living with their father, Elliott Alderson, in a tiny apartment in Sarahsville, Pennsylvania. Ann Bailey, the woman who'd been hired as a caregiver after their mother had abandoned them, was a mean-spirited woman. Ann had been changing the bed sheet and hollering and threatening Isabella with a "whooping."

Isabella couldn't understand what she had done to deserve a punishment, but whether she was innocent or not didn't matter. Ann Bailey fabricated her own grievances against the children, and she'd make damn certain they paid with a hefty punishment.

That day, she had placed Isabella into a red wagon filled with empty glass milk bottles. She'd instructed Johanna to take her sister and the bottles to the store, where Johanna was to "cash the bottles in" for five cents per bottle.

Isabella remembered that Johanna had followed Ann's instructions, grasped the wooden handle of the wagon and pulled with all of her might. Ann had remained at the end of the sidewalk, watching and smirking as Johanna began her trek with her sister. "Go on," Ann hollered, moving her hands in a fluttering gesture as if shooing a fly away. "Get going!"

Johanna tugged the handle, pulling the wagon along, but once the wagon started down the street's slope, it picked up speed. Johanna's eyes grew big and she tried to slow the accelerating wagon but the force was too great for her little arms. Screaming for Ann to help, she burst into tears as Ann stood motionless, laughing.

The wagon broke free from Johanna's desperate grasp, spiraling down the street with Isabella crying. As fast as she could, Johanna dashed after it but the wagon hit a pothole, flipped instantly, and flung Isabella and the milk bottles into the air. "No!" Johanna screamed, as her little sister landed on shards of broken glass, one piece impaling her tiny arm. Isabella wailed in pain, blood spurting and covering her shirt.

"I'm so sorry...so sorry!" Johanna cried, gathering her sister to her and trying hard to stop the bleeding with her hand. "Ann, help her!" Johanna hollered, but Ann Bailey was nowhere to be found. "Someone help my sister! Please!" Johanna shouted, and a man who had been driving by slammed on his brakes, shifted his car into park, and jumped out of the vehicle, quickly wrapping Isabella's arm with a handkerchief. "Good God," he said, "we've got to get her to a hospital fast. Her artery has been severed."

He tried to comfort the two young girls with words, but his brown eyes were grave. "You've got to let go of her," he coaxed Johanna who still held her sister to her heart. "Please let me have her. I've got to keep pressure on her wrist." His kind eyes must've won over Johanna's doubt because she released her sobbing sister into his arms. He cradled Isabella to his chest, entered his vehicle with her on his lap, and told Johanna to get into the back seat. The moment Johanna was safely inside, he sped off to the nearest hospital.

When they reached the hospital, the kind man had gotten the necessary information from Johanna and then called their father's workplace, telling him that Isabella was seriously injured. Within the hour, their father arrived, meeting the man who'd helped his daughter and even offering to buy him a new shirt since his was covered with Isabella's blood. The man refused, asking instead that Elliott buy a cheery gift for the girls who had gone through so much.

Their father had agreed, flinching a few times as he watched the doctor stitch up Isabella's severe wound and then clean the debris out of several less life-threatening ones. When he finished, he examined and cleaned Johanna's scraped hands, injuries she'd gotten from trying to hold the wagon to save Isabella.

"I'm Gabriel, by the way," the man said to their father and then turned towards the girls. "I have to go now. You two girls need a lot of rest. It's a good thing I was passing by. This could've been a real tragedy otherwise."

Johanna thanked him, her cheeks still wet with tears. Gabriel looked down at her, then cast his serious gaze towards Elliott. "She put up quite the fight to save her sister. That's some strong love there."

Agreeing, their father had walked with Gabriel into the hall and away from the emergency room. A few minutes later, the doctor stepped out of the room, leaving Isabella and Johanna alone. By themselves now, Johanna rushed to Isabella's side, her quick movements causing the wooden floor to creak as she pressed herself against the side of Isabella's bed.

"I've been waiting to talk to you alone, Izzy!" she exclaimed, cupping her hand to the side of her mouth as she murmured into Isabella's ear, "Sister, dear, bend near, so I can whisper my secret in your ear."

This was not the first time Isabella had heard her sister speak those words. Both she and Johana had developed that secret phrase to share their thoughts. Just like many times in the past, today was no different. Isabella knew that something very important would follow.

She leaned towards Johanna. "I believe that Ann wanted you to get hurt. I think that's why she put you in the wagon with all of those glass bottles," Johanna said. "She hates us for some reason. Maybe it's because she doesn't want Daddy to love us. I just don't know, but I'm so scared of what she might do next."

It didn't take long to find out.

Soon after the wagon accident, it was a day hot enough to cook an egg on concrete. Only the rich neighbors had cooling fans, which left those that didn't sick and smothered in humidity. Isabella, once again, was falsely accused of talking back to Ann, so Ann decided that Isabella needed to be punished. "Well, now, Isabella," she smirked, "You're nothing but a hot-tempered little brat. And do you know where hot-tempered little brats belong?" Not waiting for an answer, she laughed. "They belong outside in the hot sun. Now I want you to go out there and sit on those porch steps until I tell you to come in. If you dare to move from that stoop, I'll whip your behind harder and more painfully than what those broken bottles did! Do you understand me?"

Isabella nodded, too scared to utter one word. She hurried outside to the steps where she planted herself, thankful that part of the roof still shaded her.

"No! No! No!" Ann hollered to her. "Go down two more steps!"

Isabella obeyed, squinting as the full force of the sun's relentless rays beat down on her soft, pale face. She could see Johanna nearby, hiding in the shadows of the house and out of Ann's view. Immediately, relief flooded her. Johanna would help her. She'd find some way!

Soon enough, right after Ann went back into the house, Johanna arrived by her side with a flattened cardboard box that she held over Isabella's head for shade.

"I can't stand her," Johanna said, sniffing as her tears fell alongside Isabella's. "She's so mean. She makes up lies about us all the time to hurt us."

"Johanna!" a shout came from the kitchen window, and within seconds, Ann burst outside the storm door and onto the porch. "You get yourself away from her and move your ass to the back of the house if you know what's good for you! She's being punished. Leave her alone and bring that cardboard to me!"

Johanna hesitated, and Ann walked closer to where the two sisters huddled together, a switch in her hand. "You get away from her or you'll pay twice as much as she."

9

She raised the switch and Johanna ran, but only after telling Isabella she would try to find help.

Help didn't arrive soon enough.

Within a few hours, blisters had formed on Isabella's tender skin. Periodically, Ann would check on her to make certain she was still sitting in direct sunlight. "I have your sister locked in her room," she laughed. "She was trying to bring you water and food."

Another hour passed and Ann's visits stopped. Loud snoring could be heard from the living room. Isabella felt as if her skin was on fire, and crying, she touched her head as pain and darkness blanketed her.

She fell backwards against the step, and didn't remember when her father had returned from his job and found her. All she could recall was waking up in the hospital with strange people looking down at her.

"There, there now," a lady with gentle eyes said. "I'm a nurse and these aids with me are going to take care of your wounds, okay? Oh and here's the doctor with your father."

"Isabella," her father called to her. "Honey, you'll be okay. This was just an accident, right?"

"This was no accident," the doctor told him, pointing a finger at her father's chest. "This was the result of child neglect, and this poor slip of a girl now has second and third-degree burns. Once the hospital releases her, if she comes back again with so much as a scratch, I will call the police and have your children put in foster care. Do you understand?"

"Yes," her father said grimly. "It was not my doing. I love these girls. I'm a single parent, and I've been doing my best."

"This," the doctor said, gesturing with his hand across a bubbling sore on Isabella's cheek, "is not doing your best."

When Isabella returned home from the hospital, a woman that they were told to call Aunt Lottie showed up the next day. She said she wanted to spend time with the girls, and much to Ann's annoyance,

Aunt Lottie took the two girls to the local restaurant, treating them to hotdogs and their first taste of Coke-Cola.

As Johanna and Isabella were munching hungrily away, Johanna began to tell Aunt Lottie how poorly Ann treated Isabella.

"Was she responsible for her burns and the wagon accident?" Aunt Lottie asked, not looking surprised when Johanna nodded. "I thought so. She is not going to get away with this. She was hired as a maid to care for the house and you children, not harm you, and who knows what she has in her head regarding your father, but this abuse has got to stop. You can't continue to live like this."

And true to her words, Aunt Lottie took matters into her own hands and went to the house to talk to Elliott.

An argument ensued, and both girls could hear Aunt Lottie arguing that Isabella could not defend herself against such cruelty and that her protector was supposed to be her father not her sister. Elliot argued back that he could do nothing because of his job and that he needed Ann there to watch the children and take care of the house while he was away during the day.

"Then if you won't do the right thing," Aunt Lottie told him, "someone will have to. Juliana is on her way here. I imagine she'll be here within a few days, and if I were you I'd be keeping an eye on your maid because we both know what Juliana's temper is like. She would not want her girls hurt."

"Only abandoned," their father replied, his tone sounding angry.

Isabella hadn't known what he meant or who this Juliana was that they spoke about.

Three days later, however, a woman who traveled by bus from Arkansas to Pennsylvania arrived at their house with the strength of ten wildcats.

Isabella and Johanna hid under the bed when they'd heard the front door burst open and a woman shouting.

"Who is she? Can we peek?" Isabella whispered, but Johanna shook her head no. "We're safe here. Let's just see what happens."

They could hear Ann's shrill voice denying that she ever hurt the girls, and then she referred to them as little monsters and that they needed disciplining.

The argument between the stranger and Ann escalated until Ann finally admitted hating the girls. A thumping sound and crash exploded in the house with Ann screaming.

"It sounds like Ann's getting the tar beaten out of her!" Johanna exclaimed.

Police sirens shattered the outside air. A door busted open.

"The neighbors must've called the police," Johanna said. "Maybe Ann's dead. I don't hear her voice any longer." Johanna told Isabella to stay put while she peeked downstairs. She returned a few moments later. "There are policemen downstairs and Ann is not moving! They put her in an ambulance, and one of the policemen told this black-haired woman that she'd go to jail if Ann dies!"

Within the hour, their father returned home and told them that Ann was in a coma in the hospital.

"Who was the woman hitting her?" Isabella had asked him.

But he refused to answer, shaking his head. "That's not important. What's important is that because of this incident and how Ann treated you girls, the courts will take you both away from me."

And sure enough, the courts did.

A few weeks later, Isabella and Johanna walked into a big fancy room with a man sitting high above them as if he were on a stage.

"I'm Judge Wilson," he told them, "and I've looked over your home lives, young ladies, and talked with your father and the police and hospital, and I have made a decision regarding your care. You will be placed in our legal system for foster care. Your parents must prove they are fit to care for you properly if they ever want to have custody of you again."

Isabella didn't understand all of what the judge said. She knew that she only had one parent, her father, and that she'd never known anyone else since she'd been born.

"I'm going to miss Daddy," she told Johanna, leaning close.

A few minutes later, their father arrived at their sides, hugging them hard. Isabella had never seen him cry before but she saw him cry that day.

And that was the last time Isabella and Johanna would see him for a very long time.

They were whisked away by strangers and brought to a community shelter where they spent the night atop two cots and covered with wool blankets. Before falling asleep, Johanna whispered to Isabella, "Sister, dear, bend near so I can whisper my secret in your ear. You must not tell anyone because this secret is more precious than diamonds and gold and is for only you to hold."

Isabella giggled, excited to hear Johanna's secret.

"The secret is that we will be staying on a farm with dogs and cows and all kinds of fun things to do with a nice woman named Aunda. I think she is the judge's sister! I overheard a lady at the courthouse telling Daddy that we'll help this old woman work her farm and she'll help us. I heard that she's a widow who enjoys taking in children like us."

"Johanna! I hope it's true!" Isabella said, ecstatic to hear the good news. "I don't like being scared all the time, and maybe this woman is really kind and won't hit us."

"I know, Izzy," Johanna had said. "I hope so too."

At that time in their lives, they cautiously looked forward to the new life that awaited them in Zervine, Pennsylvania, but more than anything, they were relieved to be away from Ann Bailey who had taken such joy in their pain and suffering.

It didn't take long for Johanna's secret to come true. Both sisters were placed into the foster care of Aunda for several years, and Aunda was very kind, indeed.

Farm life was a lot of hard work but fun, and both girls were assigned duties until the new school year started. At 5:30 a.m. every morning, Aunda would get started on the tasks ahead for the day. After waking Johanna and Isabella, she'd have them sit on a stool and watch her as she'd milk the cows. "Learning is everything," she'd tell them in her German-accented English. "You must learn and be educated," she insisted.

When she'd finish teaching them, she'd shoo them back into the kitchen where she'd prepare a hearty meal. Eggs, bacon, homemade bread, and fresh milk were some of the most delicious food both Isabella and Johanna ever had.

"Now each of you will have different duties to tend to on this farm," Aunda told them. "When we work together, then together we can enjoy fine meals like this and even more."

Isabella soon learned that the morning task of gathering the chickens' eggs would become her duty. She enjoyed helping Aunda and tried her best to do a great job, but one morning as she was gathering eggs, a troublesome hen pecked at her toe, slicing through her delicate skin. Instinctively, Isabella swung the metal pail she was holding at the hen and connected with its head, accidently killing it.

"Please get up," she whispered to the still bird. Nudging it with a nearby stick, she begged, "Please, please get up. Don't be dead."

When the hen didn't move, Isabella started crying. What had she done? She would be in big trouble now and be punished!

Running to the house, she hurried to her room after telling Aunda that she was not feeling well.

"I'll bring your dinner up to you, honey," Aunda said, "but try to sleep until then. Maybe you are coming down with the flu. I heard it is going around in town."

Isabella stayed in bed the whole day, pretending to be sick and worrying what would happen when Aunda found the dead chicken.

When evening arrived, Aunda went outside to put the chickens away for the night, and that's when she discovered the dead hen. "Looks like we might have a disease going around in the chickens," she told the girls that night at supper. "I might have to kill quite a few that were exposed to the dead one to prevent the disease from spreading."

Isabella's heart pounded and she ran from the room with Johanna following her. She huddled near the corner of the room and started crying, inconsolable from Johanna's pleas to tell her what was wrong. Finally, Isabella wiped her runny nose and whispered, "Sister, dear, bend near so I can whisper my secret in your ear."

Johanna leaned forward and Isabella cupped her ear then said softly, "I killed that hen but didn't mean to. I tried to shoo it away with a pail."

Johanna took Isabella's hand and said, "Then we must tell Aunda what happened to the chicken. I don't think she'll be mad at all. Not like Ann." She squeezed her hand. "Please, sister. Please. You're safe. Aunda won't hurt you. And I'm here to protect you always."

Isabella said she would confess to her, and then walked into the kitchen with her head lowered and told Aunda the truth. "I'm very sorry but I accidentally killed the hen. I tried to shoo it away when it pecked my foot. Please don't punish me. Please don't hurt me."

"Oh sweet child!" Aunda exclaimed, rushing to Isabella. She hugged Isabella to her heavy skirt and frock that smelled of eggs and flour. "Of course I won't hurt you! Don't you worry one bit, child." She winked, adding, "Tomorrow we will have the best chicken dinner. Now make certain you wear shoes every time you go into the pen to gather eggs. That darn bird deserved to be whooped. It was a mean one."

And just as Aunda had promised them, they had a delicious chicken dinner the next day with all the trimmings like thick gravy, biscuits, and freshly squeezed lemonade.

As the years passed, Isabella and Johanna fell in love with the farm life and their foster mother. Every day was an adventure, whether learning a new farm task, or simply squeezing lemons for lemonade. Aunda had generously loved them and their dinners were always hearty—full of flavor and a lot of helpings so that the hunger they'd known in their short lives for love and sustenance ceased to exist.

At least for a time.

On a balmy summer day with the midday sun on her face, Isabella went for a walk on the farm. Along the walk she decided that she was going to play hide and seek from her dog, Rags. She ran into the cornfield, hiding in the lanky cornstalks, laughing as she ran down a sea of freshly tilled rows with her dog barking excitedly behind her. When she came to the end of one row, she slowly peeked out to see where Rags was. He surprised her by tugging the tail of her frock, and when she fell down, he started licking her face. Laughing, Isabella escaped his wet sloppy kisses and ran towards the house. Rags was behind her, but as the farmhouse came into sight she could see in the distance the dust rising from the arid dirt road.

That rising dust could mean only two things: there was a storm approaching or someone was on their way to visit Aunda. It was the latter.

Isabella had to find Aunda and warn her of the strange vehicle approaching. She found her filling the water buckets in the horse stalls.

"Miss Aunda!" Isabella gasped, trying to catch her breath as Rags tugged on her dress. "Hurry! There is a shiny black car coming up the lane! Who could it be?"

CHAPTER TWO

"A true sister will stand by your side."

"What's all this commotion about?" Aunda laughed, shaking her head as Isabella and Rags ran towards her.

Isabella pointed to the dust billowing from the road. "It's a black car as shiny as a new nickel! Maybe it's someone real important!"

There weren't many times since staying with Aunda that Isabella remembered the woman frowning, but at that moment, she did. "Sweet Jesus," Aunda muttered, "let's just hope it's a salesperson selling books and not the devil."

"Is everything okay, Miss Aunda? You seem upset."

"I'm fine, child," she told her, shooing her and Rags away. "Now go inside the house, find your sister, and go to your room till I call you downstairs, you understand?"

"Yes." And Isabella did just as she was told. She ran into the farmhouse, the screen door slamming behind her as she hollered for her sister.

"Isabella!" Johanna laughed, coming around into view from the icebox. "What in the world are you screaming about? What's going on?"

Isabella smiled and Johanna laughed as if expecting the next words.

"Sister, dear, bend near, so I can whisper my secret in your ear."

And Johanna did. She leaned in and Isabella whispered, "A shiny black car is here and Aunda seems upset. I think it's someone she doesn't want to see. Maybe the devil! She told me to get you and wait in our room until she calls for us."

Johanna nodded, pulling Isabella close to her neck. "I feel like there's going to be trouble, Sister, but we best hurry and get upstairs. We don't want to make Aunda mad at us. I love it here, Isabella, don't you?"

"Yes," Isabella answered, grabbing her sister's hand as they hurried to their bedroom. "Sometimes, though, I think staying with Daddy would be nice again too."

Johanna stopped, turned to Isabella, and shook her head. "No, don't say that."

"But why?" Isabella asked. "He loves us."

"Because he couldn't take care of us properly, like the judge said."

They entered their bedroom, shutting the door behind them. Every door in the farmhouse didn't close tightly all the way, and so their door was ajar a bit—just enough so that the strangers' voices could be heard.

"It's the law, Aunda Heinrich," a masculine voice said. "And I'm delivering you this notice on behalf of Zane County, PA. The probation period is now over and they can be returned. I know this must be difficult, but you have not answered the summons to appear in court. Therefore, you forced us to do this physically."

"But they are happy here! They've been here for three years. Please...."

"They don't belong here!" a shrill, shaky voice blurted out, cutting off Aunda.

"Ladies, that'll be enough," the masculine voice said again. "Keep your composure or I'll arrest you both. Aunda, I'm certain you don't want me to arrest you for obstruction, either. Now, I'm going back to the car so as to let you two have a few moments before you call the children down here."

"Oh, Johanna, I'm scared," Isabella cried, pressing her head against Johanna's shoulder. She could smell the fresh scent of Aunda's home-made soap in Johanna's frock. It comforted her a little as she blurted, "Are they talking about us? I don't want Aunda to be in trouble. That other voice sounds so mean."

"And old," Johanna added, stroking Isabella's soft hair. "It sounds like mean old Ann Bailey."

"No!" Isabella yelled, muffling a sob with her hand. "You don't think it's her, do you?"

"Shhh," Johanna soothed, rocking Isabella a little. "No, I don't think it's her. There are two more female voices downstairs besides Aunda. One definitely sounds old and mean but it's not Ann's." Kissing the side of her cheek, she said, "Don't worry, Isabella. We are safe here. The judge gave us to Aunda. And maybe later before bed, I'll tell you one of my stories you love to hear."

"Your stories are the best!" Isabella exclaimed, reaching up and putting a finger in one of Johanna's curls. "And so is your hair!" She loved the color of her sister's hair. It reminded her of the sunsets on the farm when streaks of red and orange would line the skyline.

"You're so silly," Johanna smiled, reaching up to hold Isabella's hand in her hair. "You have beautiful hair too, you know. Yours is the color of those banana-flavored popsicles Aunda treats us to every Sunday after church!"

Isabella beamed. No one ever made her feel more beautiful than her sister.

"I love you, Jo Jo," she said, using the nickname she'd made up for her long ago but only used on rare occasions.

"I love you too, Izzy," Johanna said, kissing the top of Isabella's head. "I'm glad we don't use our special nicknames very often because I never want them to lose their meaning."

"They never will."

They both giggled when Rags weaseled his way in between them to nestle his black-and-white head on Isabella's knee. For a few minutes, all that was happening downstairs was forgotten. That is, until banging erupted, then a few raised voices, and then silence.

"What do you think is happening, Johanna?" Isabella asked. "Should we go downstairs? What if it is the devil like Miss Aunda said? Maybe she needs saving!"

Rags whined, and both girls rubbed his head as if they were comforting themselves.

"Johanna? Isabella?" Aunda called from the downstairs. "Come down here, please."

Both girls could tell by Aunda's shaky voice that something was not right. Growing afraid, Isabella reached for Johanna's hand and pressed her fingers inside her sister's tight clasp. They stood up slowly, walked out of their bedroom to the top of the stairs, and paused. Looking down past the chipped banister toward the foyer, they spotted a heavy woman whose back was to them. She wore a large overcoat even though the day had been warm and sunny, and her stockings were wrinkled and partly rolled down towards the soles of her black shoes. She held a cane, pressing down on it as she leaned to the left.

Something about this old woman put more fear inside the pit of Isabella's belly than she'd ever known before. To the scary woman's right was a tall dark-haired woman who even from a distance seemed much younger.

"I don't want to walk down the steps," Isabella whispered to her sister. "I want to go to bed."

"Shhh," Johanna said, "it'll be okay." But her soothing voice sounded just as fearful as Isabella's thumping heart. "We don't have to be afraid. Let's find out what Aunda wants."

Her words were stronger than actions. Neither of them took the first step down the staircase that would lead to the next chapter in their young lives. Instead, they both stared straight ahead—not realizing that Ann Bailey was a saint compared to the woman that waited for them at the last step....

—⁄₁ᐯ—

"Hello? Is anyone home?"

Those words brought Isabella out of her childhood memories and to the present time. Forgetting briefly the staircase scene that only a few minutes ago had been branded inside her mind, she shouted, "I'm in the garden!"

"Ah, there you are," a FedEx driver said, appearing from behind the side porch and holding a medium-sized box. It was Frank, her regular delivery man, whom she'd always baked cookies for at Christmastime. "The porch screen is locked, Miss Isabella. Would you like me to place this package in the garage behind the house?"

Glancing down, she realized she still held in her hands the Lady of Shalott roses she'd snipped earlier. "I'm sorry, Frank. Yes, that'd be fine. I should've remembered you'd be here today. I'm always the last stop on your route. I just got so caught up in my garden and memories. My sister will be coming over today and I'm so excited."

"I bet you are! I still remember meeting her here one day last summer. You two were giggling like teenagers."

"We definitely do a lot of laughing at this stage in our lives. Johanna is hilarious. The wittiest persona I've ever met. I never know what will come out of her mouth," she told him, standing and straightening her spine—but her knees protested. "Ah, to be teenagers again with no aches and pains instead of halfway through life."

He laughed and shook his head. "Miss Isabella, you get around better than most teenagers. You're like unsinkable Molly. You're always doing something when I show up, and from the little I've gathered through the years, your life had never been easy, yet you found a way to push through and be successful." Winking, he shrugged. "Plus, you make the best damn cookies and peanut butter fudge *ever*."

"Johanna taught me to make that fudge."

"Your sister is a fine baker, then. You two have a great relationship, don't you?"

Isabella nodded, feeling loving tears well up from her very soul. Every part of her couldn't wait to be in the presence again of the one woman who'd been her only ally, friend, and sister. There was only one Johanna, and no one could ever replace her. "Yes, Frank," she admitted, blinking the tears away. "We do, and I can't wait to see her today. It's been a while."

"You both went through a lot together, didn't you?" he said, looking around the yard to point at the "sister-themed" rock accents, butterflies, engraved prayers, and so much more. "Did she gift you with most of these garden ornaments?"

"Many," Isabella told him, "and many I added in honor of our special relationship."

"That's how siblings should be. Not like my brother and me," he shrugged, rolling his eyes. "Anyhow, I'd better be going. You enjoy that time with your sister. I can't wait to hear about it the next time I'm here. You mentioned being caught up in memories, but you both are making new memories every time you're together."

Touched that someone besides Johanna would want to hear anything about her life, she nodded. "Very true." She waved to him as he hustled toward the front of the house after placing her package in the garage. Once she heard his truck engine rev and start down the street, she looked toward her garden once again.

"Well," she whispered to herself, looking around at the garden accents Frank had pointed out. "Should I continue remembering the past or do Johanna and I do it together when she arrives?"

A westerly breeze picked up at that moment, gently filling her lungs with the answer. It was impossible not to remember their lives from where they'd been to where they were today.

And so she tenderly snipped a few more roses and then headed inside her home. After arranging the roses in a vase to her satisfaction, she positioned them on the dining room table where she could see them from every downstairs room of her house.

The tea kettle whistled, and she quickly poured the hot water over a teabag before settling on the sofa with cup in hand. "Mmm," she smiled, sipping the soothing apple-cinnamon brew as she studied the flower pattern of the fine bone-china cup she held.

Aunda could never have afforded such luxuries such as this cup, but the flower pattern reminded Isabella of the frock Aunda wore the day Isabella and Johanna were taken from her farm.

Finishing her tea, Isabella placed the cup and saucer on the nearby coffee table, then leaned back against the cushion, closed her eyes, and continued her journey in remembrance of a time long ago—a time that should've been forgotten but was branded on her and her sister's hearts and minds every second of every day.

Misery in a person's life has a way of doing that, she thought. And so Johanna and she would never forget. Nor could they ever try to.

"Just keep holding my hand," Johanna had told her as she took a step to descend the staircase, but Isabella hadn't budged. "C'mon, Izzy," she coaxed, tugging on her hand. "Aunda is waiting."

Isabella had finally moved a little, tentatively stepping beside her sister as they descended the stairs with Rags behind them.

Aunda met them at the bottom step. Her large, loving hands that she usually kept inside her apron pockets when she was relaxed were now wringing each other. Her round brown eyes were wet, and Isabella glanced behind her to notice the heavily-clothed old woman staring back.

"You best not be looking at me like that, child, or I'll have to spank your behind," she warned Isabella, shuffling toward the steps.

"You'll do nothing of the sort!" Aunda snapped at the woman. "And if you dare ever lay a hand on them in the future, I will certainly call the police on you!"

"Now, now, no need to go and get so worked up over just a little sass," the woman said, turning toward Isabella and Johanna then back at Aunda.

"Miss Aunda," Johanna said, her voice shaking as she squeezed Isabella's hand. "We aren't leaving you, are we? We don't know these women."

"Please, Miss Aunda," Isabella cried, using her free hand to capture the hand of the woman she'd come to love. "Please don't send us away."

"That'll be enough of that," the stranger said, stepping to the side then in front of Aunda. "You two young'uns might think you're entitled to such airs after living in this fancy house with your own bedroom and nice clothes, but you belong in your stepfather's house with your real family. I am your grandmother. From now on you will call me Grandmother Swain."

"Grandmother?" both girls said in unison. "You're our grand-mother?"

There seemed to be a satisfied look of smugness in the old woman's murky hazel eyes. "I certainly am, and I've got court papers saying you are to live with my son and your mother."

"Mother?" both girls said again in unison. Isabella blinked hard. She didn't even know what a mother was. "We don't have a mother."

"Yes, girls, you do," a softer but firm voice told them, and the younger stranger stepped forward, moving her hand to take off a long-netted hat. She was beautiful with high cheekbones, red lipstick, and raven-black hair. Her narrowed eyes studied each of them. "I am your mother, and I fought hard to have you back. Now, Johanna, don't you remember me a little?" she asked, "because I know that Isabella was only an infant when I left you both."

Mother? Isabella repeated in her mind. She couldn't get that word out of her head. She and Johanna had a mother? What was a mother? She'd never known anything her entire life but her father.

Johanna remained eerily silent. Isabella stole a glance at her sister and didn't like the worried frown on her face.

"Girls, go on. You best be gettin' upstairs to gather your belongings or we'll have to leave without them. We are on a schedule, and I can tell you all about myself when we're in the car."

Rags took that moment to whine, and just hearing his moan, as if he too were devastated by the news, Isabella succumbed to a floodgate of tears. Sobbing, she ran to Aunda and threw her tiny arms around her waist. "Please! Please don't send us away! We love it here! I don't want a mother. I don't even know what one is!"

"Oh, sweet Jesus," Aunda said, her own tears flowing freely. "I'm so sorry, children. I love you like my own, but the papers they have here are legitimate. Your mother and stepfather are the rightful people who should be taking care of you both."

"No!" Johanna burst out, sprinting to Aunda and hugging her just as hard as Isabella was. "Please let us stay here."

"I said there'll be none of that!" Grandmother Swain shouted, grabbing each girl's arm to break their hold on Aunda. "Now, go on, go get your belongings. If you keep this nonsense up, you won't be taking any of them."

"That's not necessary," the younger woman who referred to herself as their mother said to the lady calling herself Grandmother Swain.

"I will not have you bullying these girls!" Aunda chimed in, angrier than Isabella had ever seen her. She pointed a finger in Grandmother Swain's face. "I can still call the police and file charges at the court for custody!"

Immediately, this stranger who was now their grandmother, softened her voice with her next words. "No harm done. No harm and no reason to get so upset. I'm only trying to get these children in their rightful place. It's been a long journey, and we are all more than a little frustrated. Certainly, you can understand that."

Aunda stepped back, shoved her hands in her apron pockets, and mumbled something that sounded like a curse word.

Neither Isabella nor Johanna had ever heard her curse before.

"Go on, sweet children," Aunda told them, her face growing pale. "Go get your things, but come here to me first." They rushed to her again and she swooped them up into a long embrace, whispering in each of their ears that she would do what she must to see them safe. After many words of love and tears, both girls hurried up the stairs to their bedroom. Rags followed, whining as if he knew it would be the last time he'd nuzzle each of their faces again.

CHAPTER THREE

"Our roots say we're sisters, our hearts say we're friends."

Life followed for Isabella and Johanna as if Aunda and her safe-haven farm never existed. Their mother's home was the first on Seventh Street. It was dark and so tiny that Isabella and Johanna were forced to sleep on the damp couch near the bathroom. Their mother and her new husband, Howard, whom she'd eloped with after abandoning Johanna, Isabella and their father, slept in the bedroom, and a galley kitchen was to the right with a tight living area and bathroom to the left. The floorboards protruded in several spots which caused splinters to puncture the girls' feet.

Right next to their house was Howard's mother's home. The girls now knew that Howard was Grandmother Swain's son and her home was a little larger than theirs but still as creepy and dark as their mother's house. What made it even worse was that Grandmother Swain's eldest daughter, Priscilla, and Priscilla's son, Junior, lived there. Both Isabella and Johanna avoided their grandmother's house as if it were a house of horrors, which often it was.

"There's no food again in the kitchen," Isabella told Johanna as both their stomachs growled loudly. "Momma keeps saying money will be coming and she'll put food on the table soon but there's nothing."

"Because she spends it with Howard when they disappear for days without telling us."

"Momma said she goes looking for work," Isabella reminded.

"Izzy, I love you so much, but sometimes you're naïve," Johanna told her, slipping an arm around her shoulders. "Do Mom and Howard ever look hungry? And where does Howard's money from working at the can factory go? They spend it on wild nights, just as the pastor warned about in church."

"I hate living here, Jo Jo, but I hate Grandmother Swain even more. Sometimes I wish she'd die. Is that wrong?"

Johanna shook her head. "No. She's cruel just like her grandson. I still have the marks on my back where she hit me with her belt."

"And you didn't even do anything wrong! She said you sassed her."

"Just like how Ann would lie so that she could hurt us. I don't know why people are that mean, but all we can do is pray and stay strong. We'll be grown up one day and we can't forget that."

"But sometimes I think we're just like those mice inside the wheel that keep spinning it and never stop. Sometimes it feels like we'll never escape these people. And Junior is just as terrible as Grandmother Swain."

Junior, who was all of ten years old, was the favorite of Grandmother Swain. On the first day of their arrival, he'd towered above them with his stocky 5'8" frame, square jaw and narrowed eyes. His brown hair was matted to his scalp as if he'd run a marathon, and his skin was pasty and flabby with his cheeks reddened as if he blushed all the time.

He'd never welcomed them, but instead, eyed them with a dark glare as if they were nothing more than despised peas and carrots on his dinner plate.

"Why do we have to have so many mean people in our lives?" Isabella had asked Johanna. After all, her older sister knew everything.

At least, that's what Isabella always believed. Johanna had just shrugged, but leaned near to Isabella.

"Because we are destined for great things," Johanna told her, "and it makes mean people want to hurt us. Don't ever let them, Izzy. The pastor said the devil uses mean people to do his work here on earth. We are going to have great lives. We are kind and good and loving. And the devil hates people as kind as us. But we must not just be kind. We must be strong, too." She lowered her voice to a whisper and said, "Sister, dear, bend near, so I can whisper my secret in your ear."

Isabella nodded and leaned in even closer.

"I think Junior is not just mean. He's evil. I saw him from the window twist the head off of a bird. Stay away from him as much as you can. Promise?"

"I will!" Isabella said, making a promise in her heart to do just as her older sister suggested. "Was the bird injured and he was just trying to put it out of its misery?"

"No. He hit it with a rock from his slingshot first, then picked it up and killed it."

Isabella shuddered. *That poor bird....* She wanted to cry. "I want to go back to Aunda's."

"Me too," Johanna said, bending to put her arms around her sister. "But we must be strong enough no matter where we are until we are old enough to leave places like this on our own."

"Okay, Jo Jo," Isabella said. "I will try."

"Now how about I tell one of my stories that you like so much?"

"Yes!" Isabella exclaimed, pointing toward the hall ceiling, then scrambling toward the ladder that led to the attic from the kitchen. "How about up there where no one will find us?"

Johanna looked up toward the ladder, walked toward the rope securing it, and gave it a tug. It moved freely. "Okay," she said. "It'll be an adventure." She pulled the rope all the way, lowering the ladder, and then she and Isabella climbed the rungs. The cluttered attic full of boxes and cedar chests were covered in inches of dust.

"Let's go over there by the window and try to prop it open for fresh air."

They moved in the direction of the front of the house with Johanna twisting the latch then trying to hoist the window upwards. After a few attempts, the aged wood gave a little and she was able to prop the window open with a nearby piece of wood.

The breeze that they'd hoped would be refreshing turned into a swirl of dust around them. Coughing and laughing, they sat down beneath the windowsill when the dust settled around them.

"Okay, now, will you tell me a story?"

Johanna laughed and nodded her head.

"But first, will you tell me if you think Momma will ever change and take care of us better?"

Johanna's eyes glistened. Isabella could clearly see the shimmer of tears on her lashes.

"Why do you always cry when I talk about Momma, Jo Jo?"

The question hung in the air before Johanna answered. "Because I think she's not a good person either, Izzy. I think she's selfish. I can't remember all of our life with her, but I remember she hurt me a few times, too. And when she saved us from Ann Bailey, she seemed like she wanted to fight more than help us. Do you remember? I heard Aunda say that Mom might have a terrible condition where she's nice one second and then really mean another."

Isabella thought on her sister's words, trying to remember, but she'd pushed those memories from her for another day. Right now, she wanted to feel cared for, loved, and hopeful of good things to come. "Can't we stop thinking of all of this bad stuff? Please tell me a story. Your stories take me away from bad memories."

Her sister studied her for a moment and then Johanna smiled and nodded her head. An ornery glint sparkled in her eyes. Isabella always loved the color of Johanna's eyes. They reminded her of the storybook she'd read in school where the pictures were of deep green grass on the hillside of a faraway country.

Johanna leaned in to Isabella. "Sister, dear, bend near, so I can whisper my secret in your ear."

Isabella giggled, bringing her hand to her mouth, giddy with expectation of what today's secret would be. "Our parents really are super rich and they live in France. Their names are Anton and Natasha. Bad people wanted their money so they fled to America, left us with kind people and told us they would return. They had to go to France to start a new life and would return to get us when they got everything settled, but we were kidnapped and are here now. But it won't be long before they return."

"And then we'll be rich and full because we will eat everything we want!"

"Everything!" Johanna laughed, twirling around a little. Her pale blue dress lifted and spun with her.

"But what about now?" Isabella asked, growing serious as her stomach rumbled again. "What can we eat now?"

"Let's go downstairs in the kitchen and look again."

Both girls hurried down the ladder, landing with a thud on the wood floor, then hoisted the ladder back up to the ceiling and secured it. Once not a trace of dust could be found on them to reveal that they had been in the attic, they ran to the kitchen, opening drawers, searching through cupboards, and finding only wax paper and baking cocoa.

"That's it?" Isabella asked, wanting more than anything to find a piece of bread, no matter how stale it would be by now. But there was nothing but what Johanna held up.

"Then let's use our imaginations and make chocolate chip cookies."

Isabella watched curiously as Johanna cut a piece of wax paper, laid it on a metal pan, then mixed cocoa with water and spread it on the paper. They only turned on the oven long enough for the mix to dry, then once it was cooled, scraped it with their fingers as if it were the finest meal.

"I'm still hungry, Jo Jo, and the cocoa is not as sweet as cookies, but that was fun."

"One day we will eat anything we want."

"When our real parents come back?"

Johanna stared oddly at her before tapping her lovingly on the head. "Yes, Izzy, and you keep thinking of my story and that'll help you get through tough times, okay?"

"How did you get so smart, Johanna? You know everything and always make me feel better."

"I wish I did know everything!" Johanna exclaimed, "but I don't. I just remember a lot from when I was allowed to go to church and nasty ol' Ann Bailey kept you home. I listened as much as I could and tried memorizing all the sermons. I know God is watching out for us, Isabella, and I know one day we won't be with these horrible people anymore. And we won't be hungry or have to sleep on the floor."

Isabella hoped Johanna was right. She wanted to believe that God was watching over them, but it seemed that God had forgotten them a long time ago. No matter what, though, she was thankful for her sister who could keep her mind on faraway lands and mansions. Every story was an adventure, and Johanna could convince Isabella about anything.

CHAPTER FOUR

*"Sisters are for sharing and wiping tears
and giving each other a hug."*

"I've never had a birthday party," Johanna whispered to Isabella a few days after their mother and Howard returned from wherever they had been. "Oh, Izzy! Can you imagine what that would be like?"

Isabella smiled, feeling her heart race with just the thought of a party. They'd be happy people there, music, gifts and food. Still, though, she couldn't see how they could have a party if they had no money.

"I don't think Momma will want one, Jo Jo. Isn't a party a lot of work and money?"

Johanna frowned, but Isabella could see that emerald-green glint that was her sister's trademark look. Whenever Johanna got that look in her eyes, she was determined about something. Grandmother Swain had told Johanna it was the look of pure mischief, but Johanna didn't seem to care. She had told Isabella that sometimes a person needed to be stubborn to get better things in life.

"Maybe I can figure something out," Johanna answered, looking as if she were adding up the hardest math in her mind. The kind of math that Isabella usually failed at in class.

A week later, their mother surprised them by telling them she was taking them to the movies.

"For real?" they'd both said in unison.

"Yes," she answered, shaking her head as if that had been a ridiculous question. "We're going to see a matinee of Roy Rogers."

"Yay!" Isabella shouted, clapping her hands, but noticing that her sister didn't seem as excited.

Their mother walked out of the room, giving them orders to wash their faces and brush their hair. When they were alone in the bathroom, Isabella asked her why she seemed upset.

"Sister, dear, bend near so I can whisper my secret in your ear."

Isabella huddled closer to Johanna, putting her ear to her sister's face.

"I invited my school class to come over tonight."

"You didn't!"

"Shhhh," Johanna said, cupping her hand over Isabella's mouth. "I don't want Momma to hear you. I thought she'd be gone with Howard this weekend! I don't know what to do."

"Oh, Jo Jo, this is terrible, but I still want to go to the movies! We've never been before. Let's go and then figure it out later."

"Hurry up!" their mother hollered from the front porch. "The movie starts soon. Get your butts in the car!"

Isabella tugged on Johanna's sleeve and they hurried toward Howard's car.

"Get in. Get in! Hurry!"

Johanna scrambled into the backseat first, and then Isabella slid on the leather seat toward Johanna, letting out a breath of air when the car rolled away without Junior. Almost every time they'd planned a family outing, Junior would somehow be invited or forced in on the activity by Grandmother Swain. Today, though, he was nowhere to be seen.

Probably killing some poor animal, Isabella thought, peering out of the window as Howard accelerated.

Glancing at Johanna's profile, she could see that her sister was worried about the party that their mother didn't know about. Throughout the movie, Johanna fumbled with her clothes and bit her lower lip until the movie's credits appeared on the screen.

Although Isabella felt sorry for her sister, she had to admit that the movie and sheer brilliance of watching something so large on screen made her forget at times what her sister had done.

It wasn't long after the movie and drive home that Johanna started to cry. "Momma, I have to tell you something."

Juliana looked at her oldest daughter and the smile she'd just worn was wiped away like a plate licked clean by the family dog.

"What in the world are you crying for?" Juliana asked, turning in the front seat to look more closely at Johanna. "Stop that, you hear? I just took you to the movies and you're crying! Do you realize how much that cost your stepdad and me tonight?"

"But I have to tell you something...."

"It can wait till we get home," Juliana said, and then as Howard pulled the Ford Torino to the curb of their home, she noticed a handful of children from Johanna's fifth grade class on the porch. "What in tarnation in going on...." Her voice trailed away as she turned back to Johanna. "Is this what you wanted to tell me?"

"I invited them over to celebrate my birthday this Sunday! I didn't think you and Howard would be home, and I've never had a birthday party before, Momma."

"Well, of all things," Juliana whispered, but her voice sounded anything but soft. When Howard parked the car, she exited the vehicle, strode up to the porch, and looked at the children holding gifts. "I am so sorry that you are all here tonight, but there's been a mistake about the date of the party. It's not this evening. I am so sorry."

Juliana smiled politely, thanking them anyway and waiting until the last child left with their parents before she turned to Johanna. "Get inside the house," she told her. "Now."

Johanna sprinted inside, and Isabella went after her but was stopped by her mother. "No," she said. "You stay here on this porch and do not leave it."

Isabella shuddered, starting to cry for her sister. She turned to find Howard who sometimes would stop bad things from happening. Several times, he'd hidden Isabella underneath a loose floorboard to the cellar when Grandmother Swain would be yelling for her, and once he'd even hidden Johanna behind some shrubs when Junior accused her of stealing his bag of Trick or Treat candy.

But now, her stepdad was nowhere to be found.

Isabella peered through a discreet part of the front window. Juliana was screaming at Johanna then slapped her in the face hard, knocking Johanna's head back. Isabella had watched chickens get killed by getting their necks twisted, and fear pumped in her body that Juliana would kill Johanna in the same way.

Please God, please... Isabella prayed, falling to her knees as the horrific sounds of Johanna getting beaten reached her ears. *I've got to help her!*

She ran inside just as her mother was shouting, "You think this is pretty and your father deserves your love?"

Juliana held a shiny new vanity mirror that their father had sent Johanna for her birthday. Slamming it against the wall, the mirror shattered into pieces, falling to the floor as Juliana took the handle and started beating Johanna with it.

Protecting herself as best she could, Johanna threw up her arms and screamed for her to stop.

"Momma! Stop! Please!" she cried. "I'm sorry! I'm sorry!" But Juliana's hand rose once again against her, and this time, finding her chance, Isabella ran between them, taking a strike meant for Johanna as Grandmother Swain appeared on the front doorway.

"Keep beating her! Don't stop!" she told Juliana. "Look at what she did! Made a laughingstock of you, that's what she did!"

"Momma, please...." Isabella said, throwing her body fully on Johanna as Johanna tried to prevent her from doing so.

"Izzy, no!" she told her. "Go hide!"

Just then, her mother calmed, dropping the mirror and slumping to the floor. She stared at Isabella then Johanna and dipped her index finger in the blood running from Johanna's scalp. "Oh my God. What have I done? I'm so sorry. So sorry...."

Grandmother Swain shuffled over, thrusting her cane toward Juliana. "You're sorry? Sorry! For what? Look what she did! She embarrassed you. Give me that thing and I'll see to it she gets the proper punishment. As a matter of fact, both girls deserve a good ass whippin'."

She shifted the weight in her legs to one side, leaned on her cane, and with her other hand tried to grab the mirror on the floor but she was too slow, and Isabella kicked her foot out, sending the broken mirror handle across the room.

"Why, you little brat!" Grandmother Swain shouted, bending down to grab Isabella but Johanna pushed her out of the way. "Hurry, Isabella! Run!"

Isabella didn't hesitate, but her sister's shove prompted her to run as fast as she could outside the house and around the back to the cellar. Grabbing the handles to the door, she swung it open, scrambled in, pulled it closed behind her, and huddled on the first step. Shielded in the dark and away from the hateful voices calling to her, she muffled her sobs with her fist so no one would hear and find her.

I hate her. I hate her. I hate her! Isabella thought, wishing that Grandmother Swain had never shown up at Aunda's to take them back to this place. And now, even worse, was that the mom she thought would protect them could be mean, too.

"Where are you, God?" she whispered into the darkness, remembering that Johanna said God was with them. "Why aren't you helping us?"

37

Soft fur touched her leg, comforting her. Isabella sniffed, breaking into a smile as she picked up Annie, a stray calico cat that had made its way to their house. "How did you get in here, girl?" she said, stroking Annie's fur. "But I'm glad you're here. Do you think that Johanna is okay? Oh Annie, I hope so!"

The darkness and Annie's presence offered Isabella comfort, but her thoughts were on Johanna's well-being and the events that led them to be brought to this place. *Why did we have to leave Miss Aunda's house? Why don't we ever have enough food? Why do we have to sleep on the couch or floor?*

After an eternity seemed to pass, Isabella could see the sun dipping below the horizon. Soon it would be completely dark except for the full moon. A harvest moon, Howard had called it.

Carefully pushing the door open, Isabella stepped outside with Annie jumping out behind her to purr at her feet.

Walking toward the front of the house, Isabella listened for any sounds but didn't hear anything alarming. She must find her sister now. Opening the screen door, she entered inside and found Johanna curled on her side on the couch, dried blood matting part of her hair. She was so still that Isabella at first became scared that she might be dead, but then she moved and Isabella let out a sigh and jumped on her.

"Shhh, Izzy," Johanna warned, "you gotta be quiet or you'll wake Momma and Howard."

"Okay, but I'm just so happy that you're alive!" Isabella whispered.

They wrapped their arms around each other and clung to one another for a long time.

—⁄ı∖—

Daylight poured through the living room window the next morning. The night had been long and dark for Isabella and Johanna, as the couch offered no real comfort and they were forced each night to make do on the worn couch where springs underneath pressed against their bodies. Many times one or both of the girls would lie on the floor, finding a tiny reprieve from the couch's discomfort until the floor's hardness offered the same.

Today, though, Johanna was being punished again for her mischief with the birthday party.

"Move over, Sis, so I can sit on the chair with you," said Isabella.

"Izzy, now, why would you want to do that? You're not the one being punished!"

"Because three hours is a long time and I'll miss you, and you told me we should always stick together no matter what."

Johanna shook her head. "This chair is hard and small. Save yourself and go outside to find your cat. Just stay away from Junior and Grandmother Swain 'cause I won't be there to protect you."

"Okay, Jo Jo," Isabella agreed, but only after her sister pointed to the door. Before leaving, though, she bent toward Johanna and kissed her cheek, noticing the red welt alongside her left ear. "I wish Momma hadn't hit you. And I wish she didn't break your beautiful mirror."

Johanna's green eyes welled up with tears, and Isabella felt bad for mentioning the mirror. "Maybe Daddy will buy you a new one."

"I don't want anything that means anything to me until we don't live here anymore, Izzy. As long as mean people are with us, we'll never have anything we love that we can hold on to."

Isabella couldn't quite understand Johanna's words. What she meant by them not being able to have anything that meant something to them. She did know, however, that her sister was really sad today, and now she had to sit on a hard chair for three hours.

Feeling like she was going to cry herself, Isabella kissed Johanna again and ran out the door to look for Annie.

"Looking for this ugly fur ball?" an all too familiar voice asked from behind her back. Isabella stopped reaching for the tool shed's door behind Grandmother Swain's house and swallowed hard. Junior was holding Annie by her neck as she flailed and curled, trying to escape his painful grasp.

"Put her down!" Isabella shouted, reaching for her but he quickly swatted down her hands with his burly one and then told her to be quiet. "If you scream again, I'll kill her right now in front of you," he warned.

Images of him snapping a bird's neck surfaced, and Isabella moaned. "Please," she begged softly, "please let her go."

"Only if you go in that shed with me and take your clothes off. It'll be really quick. I just wanna see what you look like."

Isabella had known fear most of her life, but this evil boy in front of her was some sort of terror she'd never met before. She knew he'd kill Annie in a second. And she also knew even if she did what he wanted, he'd most likely kill Annie anyway. She needed time to think. Oh, how she wished Johanna would be here or tell her what to do.

"Why do you want to see me naked?' she asked, knowing that for some reason even the boys on the school bus liked looking at magazines with half-dressed girls, but still, she needed to buy time with Junior. Maybe then someone would come out of the house looking for her, but her hopes dimmed when she remembered that Johanna was sitting on a chair and could not move.

"Well," he sneered, nodding his head toward the shed. "Go on."

Isabella moved toward the shed, and he followed, shutting the door behind them once they entered. "Go on," he said.

"How about if we walk in the woods to that open field?" Isabella asked, "because Grandmother Swain or someone else might need something in here."

At first it didn't seem like Junior was going to go with her suggestion, but then he shook his head. "You're not as dumb as you look. Yeah. Let's do that."

He squeezed Annie closer to him, and the cat screeched in pain.

Isabella wanted nothing more than to snatch her from him, but she knew that a feat like that would be impossible to achieve. Junior was so much larger, and Annie was already so fragile that she'd be dead in an instant if she tried to take her.

No, the only defense to save Annie would be to tire Junior out. He was way too heavy and out of shape for such a trek as one through Ol' Man Potter's field.

They walked in silence out around the houses to the woods and then through thick brush that opened to a clearing of miles of open fields.

"This way," Isabella said, and Junior cussed behind her but followed, his breathing more labored with every step until finally he'd had enough of walking. "That's it. We're in the clear and no one knows we're here. Now get down on the ground, but first take off your shirt and pants."

Isabella reached for the buttons of her wrinkled blouse, her fingers shaking. "I can't get this top button," she said, eyeing Annie and wishing she could communicate with her so that her next act would save them both. "Can you help, Junior?"

He rolled his eyes. "You're such a damn idiot. Okay, come closer." He put Annie down by his feet and in that split second, Isabella scooped her up, turned and ran with all her strength back to the woods and home.

Junior screamed at her, barreling after her but only managed a short sprint before he dropped somewhere behind her in a wheezing fit.

All the way home, Isabella held Annie close to her, thankful to be out of his reach and so grateful for her home that she'd always dreaded. She busted through the front door and collapsed on the couch, sobbing into Annie's fur and unable to answer her sister's questions of what had happened.

—⁊⎸⎴

Monday morning dawned with a heavy downpour as Johanna and Isabella ran to the school bus stop at the bottom of their hill. Bracing for Junior's arrival, both girls took their normal stances close to one another and clasping hands so that Junior could not get between them.

Off in the distance, a familiar car slowed then accelerated.

"Izzy!" Johanna said. "I think that was Junior in Howard's car! I wonder where they're going."

"Maybe he has a doctor's appointment."

"I don't think so," Johanna told her, pulling her along as the school bus came toward them then stopped. Once seated on the bus, Johanna smiled and looked to Isabella. "Sister, dear, bend near, so I can whisper my secret in your ear."

Isabella leaned in.

"I think Junior got expelled from our school. I heard rumors last week that he held down poor little Jimmy Carson on the railroad tracks and tried to get a train to run over him!"

"Oh, no!" Isabella cried, putting her hand to her mouth. "That's horrible. Poor Jimmy! And you know the rumor is probably true."

"If he's expelled, it's because of that or because he tried taking the clothes off another girl like he did to you, Izzy."

Isabella shuddered. "If he wasn't so fat, I wouldn't have been able to outrun him." As hard as she tried to push the memory away, it surfaced, and she remembered again. "He started to push me down into the grass so hard, Johanna, and then said he'd kill Annie if I didn't let him see me naked."

Johanna's face tightened like it usually did when she was angry. "I hate him," Johanna said, clenching her jaw. "I hope one day he's punished for all he's done."

"That'll never happen!" Isabella said, rolling her eyes. "He's Grandmother Swain's favorite. She'll protect him forever."

"Well," Johanna pointed out, "she can't live forever, so maybe we'll see him get what he deserves—and her too before she dies."

Isabella agreed, and their day continued as usual, each of them attending their classes. But then, as the day progressed, the whispers that had been hushed throughout the day began to grow louder in the school building's corridors.

"Did you hear what Junior did?" some whispered.

"He's going to go to jail!" others guessed.

"Poor Jimmy Carson! He's got bruises all over him and a gash in his head the size of a fifty-cent piece!" some children told anyone who'd listen.

The school was buzzing with rumors about Junior trying to kill a handicapped boy.

When the girls arrived home later, their momma was waiting for them in the kitchen. Her movements were quick and forceful, a telltale sign that she was agitated about something. Isabella's stomach tightened. *Please, God, don't let her be mad at Johanna again.*

"I've made a bowl of mashed potatoes," she told them, "because we're eating supper with Grandma tonight. Aunt Priscilla is back in town and we are celebrating."

"No!" Johanna blurted out, her green eyes wet with tears. "Please, Momma, can't we stay here while you and Howard eat there?"

"Absolutely not, Johanna! And Isabella, don't you go gettin' any foolish ideas in your head, either. We're all eating together tonight. Now both of you, go wash your faces and hands so we can be on our way."

43

Both girls immediately obeyed, feeling as if they'd been punched in their stomachs.

"We can do this, Izzy," Johanna said, tugging her hand to pull her alongside as they made their way to the dark, damp bathroom. "We just have to stick together while there. Okay?"

The tears in Johanna's eyes glistened, and Isabella felt her own spring forth. "Why do you think God gave us to such a terrible family, Jo Jo?"

Johanna grew silent as she turned on the sink's faucet. The water was always brown when it first began to flow, and Isabella hated how it looked and smelled.

"I don't know what God was thinking, but I don't think he ever wanted us to be treated like we are. I think, Izzy, we just need to believe like the pastor says and remember that God will help us out of trouble."

"I sure hope so," Isabella said, shoving her hands under the brown water, "because He sure does seem far away when trouble is right next door.

CHAPTER FIVE

"It was so nice growing up with my sister, someone to lean on, someone to count on...someone to love me."

Grandmother Swain's house looked just as evil as Grandmother Swain and Junior. Decorative pots filled with shrubs nestled on the porch did nothing to warm the chill one felt when stepping over the threshold. Although most of the row houses were designed architecturally like the others on the street, Grandmother Swain's house stuck out because, if one studied it from across the road, the peaked roof in several places looked high and dark like the devil's horns.

How fitting for someone so evil, Isabella thought as she and Johanna followed their mother up the porch steps, over the threshold, and into the mean ol' woman's house.

"It's about time," Grandmother Swain greeted them, sitting at the kitchen table with Junior to her left and Priscilla to her right. "You people act as if I live five miles down the road instead of right next to you. What took so long?"

"The girls took too long in the bathroom cleanin' up," their mother said, tugging their hands forward and practically pushing them both to sit in the empty chairs at the table.

"Momma!" both girls said in unison, wanting to defend themselves that it actually wasn't they who delayed the dinner but their mother and Howard enjoying a cigarette. Instead they kept quiet.

"Then sounds like they deserve a whippin' for such pride," Grandmother Swain said, studying each girl with eyes so beady that once in a while Isabella had to be certain she even possessed eyes. At those times, she'd look closely when Grandmother Swain's head was turned, and then she'd spot them—tiny slits containing eyes that no doubt were black.

"There will be no "whippin'" for them," Juliana told her mother-in-law, placing the bowl of mashed potatoes on the table with a thud, then giving Priscilla a hug. "Not like you used to do to Howard."

Junior snickered, and both Isabella and Johanna lifted their heads to look at him. His pudgy cheeks were spotted red, and his thin lips were wet with spit from a constant habit of licking them. Just like a pig in front of a slop bucket filled with grain.

"I think Junior here is wanting to laugh at what you just said, Juliana," Grandmother Swain said, moving to the side to pick up her cane and then rapping it on the floor as if for dramatic effect. "Because if memory serves me right, even though I'm old, I can remember a short while ago where you beat the tar out of this young'un.""

Now Junior gave way to a full laugh and Grandmother Swain joined in.

Juliana's face reddened, whether with anger or embarrassment, and she mumbled a few curse words then said, "Are we going to eat or just sit around and badger each other? I'm sure Priscilla here is wanting to eat. That bus trip from Philly is awful."

"Damn right it is," Priscilla finally chimed in after what seemed like a long silence since they had arrived.

Isabella and Johanna had heard plenty of stories about their Aunt Priscilla. Mostly that she liked men and that whenever the wind blew, she'd have another one that she'd take off somewhere with, leaving Junior to be raised by Grandmother Swain.

Not that the old witch seemed to care because she seemed ecstatic to create a clone just as mean and ugly as she was.

"Where's Howard?" Priscilla asked, dumping a spoonful of mashed potatoes on her dish. "Does he work tonight?"

"He's not feeling well," Juliana replied, reaching for the copper pot of baked chicken.

By the time all the adults and Junior served themselves from the bowls, there was little food left for Johanna and Isabella. Just like always.

Both had always wondered if Grandmother Swain cooked so little on purpose just to tease them with the delicious aroma of baked chicken, fresh corn and apple pie, but not enough for them to even whet their appetites.

And no one but the two girls seemed to care.

Their mother was too busy in her own world to pay much attention to them. Their Aunt Priscilla was rarely around, nor did she seem at all interested in her nieces either. And then Junior and Grandmother Swain, well, they were plain devious—looking for ways to get them in trouble, and when those ways didn't work, they would make offenses up just to see them punished.

Isabella caught Junior staring at her and turned away. Johanna reached for her hand under the table then leaned in. "Sister, dear, stay close to me tonight. Remember."

"No whispering at the table," their grandmother scolded. "Maybe you two have too much time on your hands. Best put those idle hands to use. You both can take the plates away and begin washing them."

"But we're not done with our dinner," Johanna said, looking down at the miniscule amount of food she had left.

"There's hardly enough there to feed a rabbit," Junior laughed, stuffing another hefty fork of mashed potatoes into his mouth. "You best be doin' what our grandmother says."

"Don't be telling my children what to do, Junior," their mother said, and her defense brought a spark of hope to Isabella's soul. Until their grandmother stood up, leaned on her cane, and shook her head.

"What's the matter with you these days? Have you gone daft? Those girls of yours need to learn a solid work ethic and discipline."

"Please! Do we have to argue about every damn thing in this house?" Priscilla exclaimed, and all turned toward her. Her black eyes were even darker now, smudged with eyeliner, and her raven-colored hair was slightly damp from sweat and the lack of air circulating through the house. Grandmother Swain liked things hot. Said she was too cold all the time and forbade anyone to open the windows or prop the door open for a breeze.

Every day in her house was hot, but tonight was extra stifling.

"Okay, okay," Juliana said, and her tone suggested that she'd given in to the demands of her mother-in-law. Turning toward her daughters, she told them, "Go on. Do what your grandmother wants, but be careful not to break anything."

"They best be not breakin' my dishes."

And those words are what exactly Johanna and Isabella knew their grandmother wanted to happen. That way, if they did break something, they'd pay dearly.

"I hate her," Isabella whispered low again as they filled the kitchen sink with soapy water. "I wish we never left the farm. We were never hungry there." She pushed her hands in the hot water, grabbed the washcloth, and started washing the first dish while Johanna waited beside her to dry it. "At least Momma stood up for us!"

Johanna fisted the dish towel, her eyes dark. "Don't think for one minute that Momma actually cares about us, Izzy! She does not. Haven't you realized yet that all she cares about is her pride? Like she never defends us or takes care of us in any way other than to stop someone from ordering us about or hurting us—like that wicked Ann did. But I don't think it's because she loves us. It's because she's prideful and doesn't like people telling us what to do over her."

Isabella paused her washing for a moment. Johanna knew almost everything and sometimes she seemed much smarter. Like now. Isabella didn't know what all of that meant, like her mother being prideful, but if Johanna said it, it must be true. Still, though, sometimes it was hard not understanding all the secrets of the world like Johanna could.

"I don't know what all that means, Jo Jo," Isabella admitted, turning toward the sink again, "but if you say it, I believe it."

"One day it will make sense, but until then just try always to stay close to me."

"You and Annie are the only things I have that love me. I will stay close."

Just then, loud voices erupted in the living room. Johanna and Isabella looked toward the others and found Priscilla holding a newspaper toward Junior. "It says Jimmy Carson is in the hospital due to an accident on the train tracks and that the police had to pry him free! Did you have anything to do with this?"

"How dare you accuse this child!" Grandmother Swain butted in, swatting the newspaper to the ground from Priscilla's hands. "You come here from being gone for months and the first thing you do is accuse your son? You know damn well that this community is jealous of our Junior! He gets blamed for everything illicit that happens here."

"Jealous of what exactly?" Juliana laughed. "We are talking of Junior, right?"

"Okay! Don't start on my son now," Priscilla warned, turning toward Juliana. "I'm glad to be back home and all, but it's me, his mother, who's the only one allowed to talk like that about him."

Johanna pressed her elbow gently into Isabella's side. "See?" she whispered. "That's pride. She doesn't care about Junior, just who's disrepectin' her."

And suddenly, Isabella understood.

The room grew hotter as Grandmother Swain raised her cane. "That's enough caterwauling!" she shouted, and after a few coughs, her voice became shaky but not shaky enough to stop her from berating her Priscilla and Juliana. "I didn't have dinner here tonight so everyone can be pickin' on Junior. He's a good boy. And go ahead, ask him. Ask him again if he had anything to do with that stupid Jimmy Carson's accident."

Priscilla's eyes narrowed a bit and she shook her head. Turning toward Junior, she asked, "Did you have anything to do with his accident? That's the first thing I was told when I stepped off of the bus today. Now you best be tellin' me the truth, you hear?"

Within seconds, Junior busted out crying. Throwing his glass of milk against the wall, he screamed through tears and snot. "No, I didn't! And I hate you! I hate this town! I hate Jimmy Carson and I hate those stupid brats in the kitchen! I bet they started the rumors! I hate you all for even thinking I had something to do with it! Everyone hates Jimmy Carson. He's dumb as a brick and slow as Uncle Howard's car with his ugly leg braces. I think it's great what happened to him but I didn't do it!"

Grandmother Swain rushed over to him as fast as she could for one who was basically crippled. Grabbing his head to her chest, she soothed him as if he were an infant.

"There! Are you satisfied now?" she asked her daughter, but Priscilla was already apologizing to her son as she reached for his hand.

Both Isabella and Johanna had just witnessed manipulation at its finest, although they both knew that Grandmother Swain had set up this moment. She most likely had told Junior what to say and how to act, and she most likely had told him to incriminate both of them.

"We are going to go home now," Juliana announced, calling for the girls who were still in the kitchen. They'd only gotten half of the dishes washed and told their mother that fact, hoping they wouldn't be punished.

"Don't you dare take those girls home without them finishing," Grandmother Swain said, looking up at their mother and then sweeping her gaze toward the girls. "And they best be cleanin' up that broken glass and milk." Her eyes turned into slits and paused on them as if a predator sizing up its prey.

"I'll take them home if I want," their mother said, "but in this case, since you've gotten your hands full with this other child, I'll let one of them stay."

"Keep Isabella here!" Junior suggested, gazing up through his tears to turn his head toward his cousins. Most likely, the only two people who saw a smirk appear were the two girls. "She was mean to me the other day and deserves it the most," he added.

Isabella grew still, her heart pumping as if a bird trapped in a cage. Johanna slipped an arm around her waist and whispered, "Remember, you said you'd do what I say. So just keep quiet." She then turned to their mother. "I finished my homework and Isabella didn't, Momma. I can stay."

Their mother only took a moment to think about it and then she agreed. Junior let out a huff, apparently disgusted with her decision.

As Juliana pulled Isabella's hands toward the door and over the threshold, Isabella couldn't help but feel as though she'd just left her sister in hell. Crying softly, she did the only thing she could. She prayed for her.

CHAPTER SIX

*"I never try to make anyone my best friend because I already
have one and she is my sister."*

"Is that all that happened, then?" Isabella asked Johanna the next
day as they walked to the school bus stop. "He fell asleep on the
couch?"

"Yes!" Johanna smiled, filling her in on the details. "I finished the
dishes and left before Grandmother Swain could get back from the
bathroom."

"Oh, Jo Jo! I am so happy. I prayed for you," Isabella told her, a
thread of hope sprouting within as if maybe God hadn't forgotten
them after all.

"Well, let's keep praying, Izzy," she said, and then when they
spotted the bus stop ahead, Johanna placed her arm on Isabella's
shoulder to stop her from walking. She bent close. "Sister, dear, bend
near, so I can whisper my secret in your ear."

Giggling, Isabella leaned in.

"There's two secrets. The first is, I heard last night Grandmother
Swain telling Aunt Priscilla that Junior did get expelled from school
because the school believed the rumors about him trying to kill
Jimmy Carson. The second secret is I heard Momma talking to
Howard this morning, and I think Daddy is coming to get us and
take us to live with him and his new wife! Her name is Estelle."

"Really?"

"Yes!" Johanna said, and then she started walking again after reaching for Isabella's hand. "Momma told Howard that she wasn't going to argue with him, and then decided it would be better if we went to live with Daddy because I was too bad and she couldn't control me."

"But that's a lie!"

"I know," Johanna said, "but Momma is trying to make herself feel better because I think she decided that she and Howard can leave more often if we aren't around."

The excitement Isabella had just felt waned some. Why was it that no one in their own family wanted them, but the person that did, that wonderful woman, Aunda, couldn't have them? Why did mean people like Junior receive love, yet they never got any affection?

As if sensing Isabella's grim thoughts, Johanna hugged her. "Only God knows why we're treated the way we are, Izzy. But we have each other and we can get through anything with God helping us and if we stick together. We have to be strong and make something of ourselves one day."

"Sometimes I don't think it could get worse," Isabella confided, finding comfort in the scent of her sister's hair. Jo Jo always had the best scented hair ever since finding a half-used bottle of their mother's perfume behind a dresser. She only applied it after they left the house so that their mother wouldn't take it back, and many times she let Isabella dab a bit of the floral fragrance on her wrists.

The school day progressed in an excited fashion. Both girls learned that, indeed, Junior had been expelled. They'd talked about it throughout the day until arriving home later where the house was empty once again.

"Where do you think everyone is? Grandmother Swain's house looks empty too."

"I don't know," Johanna said, throwing her books down on the couch. "Maybe they left us for good. Wouldn't that be great? We could go back to Miss Aunda's."

Isabella thought about it for a moment, but the mere possibility put a dull ache inside her stomach. She'd never longed for anything more in her entire life, and each night she closed her eyes and imagined Johanna and her back on the farm where they were loved and cared for.

"Stop looking so sad or you'll make me sad," Johanna said, reaching for Isabella's hair and tugging a lock. "If Momma would let you wash your hair more often, it would shine like silky spun gold."

Isabella reached a hand up and touched her hair. "Do you think so?" she smiled, remembering that it had shone more brightly at Aunda's farm. "But Momma won't let me 'cause she says it takes too much water."

"Grandmother Swain put that thought in her head," Johanna told her, walking toward the kitchen pantry. "She told her that the well can dry up, but our other neighbor said it never has dried up in fifty years and won't now. Grandmother Swain just wants you to go to school with stinky hair so that the kids will make fun of you. She doesn't know that I spray mine or that we wash it in the creek behind ol' Man Johnson's farm when it's warm."

Isabella frowned. *So that's why she rarely was allowed to bathe at the house.*

When Johanna opened the door to the pantry, it was bare again of food. She found only an empty preserve jar, a broken mousetrap, and a box of corn starch.

"This cabinet is about as empty as Grandmother's heart," Johanna said, shutting the door and turning toward Isabella. "I hope Daddy comes for us. At least he'll make sure we have food often."

"Do you want to spread cocoa on a cookie sheet and bake it like we did before?"

"There's not even cocoa," Johanna answered, gazing around the kitchen.

Just then, the front door opened, and their mother and stepfather barged in, unaware that the two girls were in the kitchen.

"He's not getting them unless he pays me," their mother was saying, her high-pitched voice shaky. "What does he think? That we're just made out of money and that we're able to afford taking care of them?"

Howard mumbled something that apparently riled up their mother. "I did not blow all that money on gambling!"

The door opened again, and Howard must've walked out because their mother entered the kitchen by herself.

She paused for only a surprised second when she saw both of her daughters looking at her. "How long have you been in here?" she asked, and then shook her head, her black hair falling softly around her shoulders with the gesture.

Isabella always thought her mother and Johanna were the most beautiful-looking women in the world, but she would never again think their mother truly cared about them. Not after the way she beat Johanna.

"Never mind," her mother said. "I don't want to know." She walked to the sink and turned the faucet on. "I'm glad you both are here anyway. I have something to discuss with you."

Johanna reached for Isabella's hand, squeezing it gently as if to say "I told you so. Daddy must be coming for us."

"You know how much I love you two, but I can't keep putting up with your rebellious nature, Johanna, or how you're always getting under Grandma and Junior's skin, Isabella."

Both girls kept silent, learning early on to keep quiet with people who would harm them.

"And so," their mother continued, waving her hands in the air as if for dramatic effect, "I've decided that your father needs to be doing his part. Since he's married now, you both will be living with him and his new wife, Estelle."

"When will they come for us?" Johanna asked, and their mother shook her head. "Most likely tomorrow morning."

"Can I take Annie? Please?" Isabella said, fighting back tears if the answer was no.

"You and that damn cat. That's up to your father. You can ask him tomorrow."

It seemed like a thousand questions flooded Isabella's mind at once. Did their mother ever love them? Would they ever see her again? And what of school? Would they pass if they left now?

"Isabella, quit looking like I just whipped your behind, and Johanna try to hide that smirk that shows how happy you are to be leaving here."

Isabella cast a shy glance toward Johanna. Yup. Her sister was smiling. In the last few years, she'd begun to see all the things she loved about Johanna come out to others. Johanna's courage and her wisdom and even how sometimes she didn't care if something she said caused her to be punished—she'd say it anyway.

Johanna was everything she was not, but maybe one day she could be more like her.

Their mother didn't have much more to say; she just instructed them to pack up their belongings in the morning in two milk crates they'd find on the outside porch.

Both girls knew they'd not need anything larger. They each only owned three dresses and a nightgown and one pair of shoes.

"Do you think Daddy will let me keep Annie?" Isabella asked Johanna later that night as they lay pressed against one another on the living room floor for warmth.

"I hope so," Johanna whispered, shivering when the draft underneath the front door kicked up even worse. "And I hope Estelle is nice, but anything should be better than living here."

"Should we pray?" Isabella asked. "I know I've asked you about God before, but do you think God doesn't like us for some reason?"

Johanna sighed. "Well, he answered your prayer when I was left at Grandma's the other day. And he helped you escape Junior and save Annie. So, of course, we should pray. We have a lot to be angry about because of what people have done to us, but we shouldn't be angry at God. He hasn't done anything bad. It's some people that are bad."

"Okay, Jo Jo," Isabella said, pondering over her sister's words. "I trust you. I will try hard not to be mad at God. And I will pray."

Johanna kissed the top of her head. "My beautiful sister, one day you'll see all things like I do. And you won't be so afraid of people anymore. You'll start getting braver as you get older. Just like you were with Junior. That took a lot of courage and a lot of smarts."

"You think so?" Isabella asked, wanting desperately to believe that she wasn't as stupid as she'd been told most of her life.

"Absolutely," Johanna said. "Don't ever let what others say make you believe they're right. You're smart, pretty, and kind, and they're mean, ugly, and stupid."

Isabella laughed. Johanna certainly had a way of making her think differently.

"Johanna, will you always stay with me? I never want to be separated from you, and sometimes the future scares me when I think of you getting older and maybe leaving me one day."

No sooner had she said the words than she began to cry. There wasn't much she loved in life. Johanna, Annie, Rags, and Miss Aunda were the only beautiful things she had memories of. And out of all of them, Johanna surpassed them all. Life without her would not be fitting to live.

"I will never ever leave you, sister dear," Johanna assured her, hugging her to her and squeezing hard. "We only have each other, and I will always take care of you, no matter what. I'll never leave you."

Isabella wiped her tears away, sniffed, then closed her eyes. Johanna was near, and she didn't have to worry about the future anymore because her beautiful sister would always be in it.

"Goodnight, Izzy."

"Goodnight, Jo Jo."

"I love you."

"I love you, too."

And both fell asleep, pushing thoughts of the future and their father, their mother, grandmother, and Junior from their minds, for they had each other. And for that moment, life was peaceful and promising, even if they were cold and hungry and lying on a splintered wooden floor.

CHAPTER SEVEN

*"I never try to make anyone my best friend because I already
have one and she is my sister."*

Saturday morning dawned as uneventful as all the days before. Same yellow-orange sun in the east, same traffic on the dirt road, and the same feeling as if their lives would be forever trapped in the horrid little house on Seventh Street.

Each hour brought renewed angst for Isabella and Johanna as fears surfaced that their father would not arrive for them.

"Do you think he changed his mind?" Howard said, pouring a cup of coffee for Juliana.

Juliana sat at the kitchen table, her hair and makeup fixed as if she were performing in a Broadway show. She'd made the girls not only pack their own belongings, but she'd had them scrub the house so she'd make a good impression and wouldn't look like some lowlife when her ex-husband arrived.

Tired from their cleaning duties, both girls sat on the couch with Isabella leaning into Johanna to rest her head.

"Do you think he's coming?" she asked her.

Johanna nodded. "Yes, I do. He's probably just delayed."

"Do you think we'll like Estelle?"

"I hope so."

"Do you think she'll be like the wicked stepmother in Cinderella?"

"Good grief, Izzy," Johanna said, pushing her slightly away to look at her. "I don't know, but I doubt it. I've heard good things about her and I shared those with you."

"But what if she changes?" And then Isabella leaned in closer for only Johanna to hear her next words, "Like Momma did?"

"Then we'll run away."

Isabella's eyes widened. She'd never heard Johanna say anything like that, but somehow, the thought didn't scare her. Maybe it was because their lives had been so bad already that running away couldn't be any worse.

And maybe they could run away to Miss Aunda's.

Isabella smiled. She was all of nine years old now, and soon she'd be an adult who wouldn't need to be with mean people any longer. Only Johanna.

"He's here!" their mother hollered from the kitchen, peeking over the sink and through the window facing the street. "Well, where would he get the money for such a fancy car?"

Quickly, both girls moved to the front screen door, watching as a black Ford rolled down the street, pulling to the curb in front of their house and parking there. Isabella squealed in delight, muffling her enthusiasm as best as she could with her hand. "Maybe he's rich now. And look, I think our new momma is with him!"

"She's *not* your new mother," Juliana snapped, walking over toward them. "You have only one mother and that's me. Don't forget it."

"Yes, ma'am," Isabella said, not wanting to be reprimanded any longer by the person who should've loved them.

"Good," Juliana whispered, turning her gaze back toward the front window where Elliott and Estelle could be seen walking toward the porch steps. Their dad appeared as handsome as ever with dark hair, tall in stature but broad as well—his face stern but attractive with thick eyebrows and blue eyes that some family members referred to as more beautiful than the sea.

Isabella had always wished she'd had Johanna's green eyes, but now, looking at their father, she realized that although Johanna's eyes were more beautiful, at least Isabella possessed something of someone who'd been kind to them.

She hoped her father hadn't changed.

"She looks nice," Johanna whispered to Isabella. "And she's pretty in a kind of teacher-like way. What do you think?"

As their father talked with their mother and Howard, Isabella peered shyly at Estelle. The older woman was tall, taller than their mother, with a slim build. A netted hat, positioned stylishly, shadowed part of her face, and she had high cheekbones just like actresses Isabella had seen in the movies.

"She's pretty," Isabella whispered, hoping that one day she could try on that expensive-looking hat.

"Pretty on the outside means nothing unless she's the same on the inside," Johanna said, reaching for and then squeezing Isabella's hand. "Come on, let's go introduce ourselves."

They walked toward their mother and Howard who was talking with their father and Estelle.

"I am not going to pay you for any expenses you think you've incurred since caring for our daughters," their dad was saying. "They are your children, too, and I'm not going to be harassed into thinking that I owe you a penny."

Isabella looked at her mother. She'd only seen her that angry another time, and that had been when she'd been beating Johanna.

"Johanna, come here," he said to Johanna.

Isabella would not let go of Johanna's hand but walked with her sister to their father.

He stooped down some and lifted Johanna's chin up with his fingers, studying her. He then looked up to their mother. "Is this how you think you deserve a reward?" he asked, his cheeks red as he stepped forward, but Estelle put her hand on his arm. "You deserve money for slapping around our daughter?"

Juliana cursed, then tried to explain that Johanna's discolored and fading bruises were a result of an accident. By the silence in the room, she must've quickly picked up that no one was believing her, as she then proceeded to justify her actions.

"I'm not interested," he told her, kneeling down a bit and motioning for his daughters to come into his arms.

Isabella didn't need encouragement. She rushed into his arms and he hugged them both to his chest. "You both have grown so much!" he exclaimed, kissing the tops of their heads. He then moved back some and looked toward his new wife. "Girls, I'd like you to meet your stepmother, Estelle. I think you're going to love her just like I do."

Johanna smiled, but wary to approach Estelle, she just stood where she was. Isabella followed her lead but was surprised when Estelle closed the gap between them by walking over quickly and putting her arms around them both.

"It's so wonderful to meet you both," she said, her voice pleasant. "I've heard so many great things about you."

Isabella grinned, liking her already, and she turned toward her sister who was smiling too.

Butterflies escaped her stomach. *Maybe, just maybe, the bad part of their lives was over now. Now, if only she could get a moment with her father to ask about Annie...*

"Is this all you have?" their father asked, looking down beside them at their belongings.

"Daddy, can I—" Isabella started, but her mother cut her off by engaging him in conversation again about money. He mumbled something that must not have been very nice because their mother's face contorted into an angry frown.

"They've been taken care of as best as I could, considering that I'm broke."

"From gambling no doubt," he said, motioning for the girls to give their mother a hug and then head outside toward his car. Isabella hugged Juliana, but Johanna walked toward the front door.

Isabella soon followed, hoping for another chance to talk with their father before they left.

"Girls, hold up," Estelle called to both of them, following them outside.

They stopped and turned toward her. Their new stepmother walked toward them, her hands behind her back as if in a leisurely stroll. She stopped in front of them, tilted her head, and her delicate hat lifted some to reveal soft brown eyes. "Is there anything else you've forgotten?"

"No," Johanna said, her green eyes bright as she shyly studied their new stepmother.

"Really?" Estelle smiled, "how 'bout this? Did you forget this?"

She brought her hands to the front and Annie lay perfectly in the woman's hands as if it was the most contented place to be.

"Annie!" Isabella shouted, and the kitten jumped down and purred by her feet. Scooping her up and bringing her to her chest, she looked at Estelle. "She can come?"

"Absolutely."

Isabella threw her arms around her new stepmother, squishing Annie a little, but the little fur-ball didn't seem to mind.

Johanna smiled too, thanking Estelle, and then all three nestled inside the car with Annie on Isabella's lap.

Their father returned soon enough, his face stern, as if he'd just had another argument with their mother.

Before scooting into the driver's side, he turned and gazed down at Annie on Isabella's lap and then toward Estelle. She smiled and shrugged. Immediately, he smiled too, and Isabella let out a sigh.

"Sister dear, bend near, so I can whisper my secret in your ear."

Isabella leaned into Johanna's shoulder. "I think Estelle is nice," Johanna said, "and I heard Momma telling Howard this morning that Daddy said he never wants us to go back to her house. Ever."

Just then, as their father started the car, the sun peeked from behind dark clouds, shining its brightness on the road ahead and their new journey.

Isabella closed her eyes and breathed deeply.

She hoped it was a sign that her and Johanna's lives would always stay sunny.

CHAPTER EIGHT

*"A sister is a special angel on earth who brings out
your best qualities."*

When Isabella and Johanna arrived in Irvine, Pennsylvania, where their father and Estelle lived, their eyes widened in disbelief. The two-story brick house had dormers, black shutters, and a yard that was so large—a swing set was positioned squarely in the middle.

Isabella squealed and nudged her sister. "Johanna! Look!"

"I see," Johanna said, appearing unaffected by the sight before them, but her eyes were just as wide.

Their father got out of the car, walked toward the passenger side, and then opened the door for Estelle. After she exited the vehicle, he helped the girls by first taking Annie and handing her to Estelle and then gathering their belongings. Finally, he gave them each a hand and helped them out of the back seats.

"Welcome home," he said, and they both looked at him.

His face seemed more relaxed than Isabella had ever remembered seeing it. It had been years since she'd seen him, but she could still remember that his eyes were always red, as if he didn't get much sleep, and his features seemed older back when she'd been with him.

Now, he appeared healthier and happier too, especially by the way he looked at them. As if he'd truly missed them.

"Girls," he told them, motioning for them to follow. "Come meet your stepbrother and stepsister."

Johanna gasped as their father opened the door. Two other children, a pleasant-looking boy with red hair, blue eyes, and a muscular build, and a black-haired girl ran towards them. Crowding them with questions and hugs, Isabella laughed as Annie meowed loudly.

"Whoa!" Estelle said, coming up behind them all. "Why not introduce yourselves first?"

"Hello," the boy said, laughing and stepping back a bit. He looked at both Isabella and Johanna. "I'm David, your brother, and this is Wanda, your other sister. You also have another sister, Stella, and she's just a baby! Wanna see her?"

Both Isabella and Johanna nodded, following David and Wanda up a small staircase to the landing and then stopping at what would be their new room. David put their belongings near a large bed, then motioned for them to follow him and Wanda down the hall. They stopped at a larger room where Isabella guessed was her father's and Estelle's bedroom. Near the neatly made bed was a bassinet.

"You gotta be quiet," Wanda whispered, tiptoeing towards the crib.

They all followed her lead. When they reached the white-tipped bassinet with ruffles and lace, Isabella peered in. Staring back at her with a grin was the most beautiful baby she'd ever seen. Not that she'd had a lot of experience with babies, but in church she'd always be looking at them nestled in their mothers' arms or hanging on their mothers' hips. Isabella had usually spent the whole church service trying to get them to laugh, and now she was face to face with not only a beautiful baby but another sister as well.

"Hello, baby Stella," Isabella said, and asked David and Wanda if she could touch Stella's hand.

"You can do more than that," Wanda giggled, pushing her hands gently underneath Stella to lift her up and cradle her a moment.

She then handed her to Isabella. "You can hold her." And then she proceeded to tell her how to do just that.

Isabella had never held a baby before. She immediately fell in love. During the days that followed, she'd play Peek-a-Boo with Stella, getting her sister to laugh. The days became brighter and harmony seemed etched into every recess of the house, so much so that Isabella began excelling in school.

"We are so very proud of you," Estelle told her one evening after dinner. "I don't know one person who wouldn't be."

Johanna leaned in and whispered, "I am proud of you too, Izzy. I wish I had your brain and determination to push ahead in all those tough subjects like Geometry."

Isabella warmed to everyone's affection, feeling as though it was a beautiful dream. If everyone was happy for her, maybe her mother would be too.

"I know what you're thinking," Johanna said the next morning before heading to the school bus, "but don't fool yourself. Momma would not be proud. She's too selfish."

Isabella didn't know how Johanna always seemed to know what she was thinking, but this time, she didn't spend much effort finding out. Instead, even though she appreciated her sister's wisdom, she decided she'd send their mom a copy of her grades. For several weeks, she snuck a letter with her grades to the post office, but Juliana never acknowledged she'd received them.

"Damn it, Izzy," Johanna said after catching her returning from the post office. "Why do you care so much about Momma's approval? You might be smart in school but don't be dumb about people."

Isabella just shrugged, determined to see if somehow she could win her mother's pride. The next day, Saturday, dawned beautifully with a clear sky and spring air. As was becoming the norm, David, Johanna, Wanda and Isabella would walk to the theater house a few blocks from their house.

This time, when the movie ended and they were walking home, Johanna wanted to stop at Higbee's Department Store to ride the escalators. David was against it, knowing that he was put in charge of his sisters, but Johanna insisted.

"Okay," he finally agreed, but we have to be home by 4 o'clock.

They entered the store with Johanna squealing in delight as she viewed the "moving stairs." She rode them up and down and continued to do so long after her brother and sister became bored.

"We've got to go," Wanda told her, but Johanna shrugged her warning off. "Johanna, David has baseball practice. He's the best pitcher on the team and the coach will be mad if he doesn't show up. We have to go!"

When Johanna went back on the escalator, David said to his two other sisters that they were going to leave without her.

Isabella hesitated but Johanna waved her on.

When they arrived home, the first question Estelle asked was to Johanna's whereabouts.

"You know very well you are to look out for your sisters, David!" Estelle said. "Elliott will be home soon so I guess he can handle this mess."

Later when Elliott arrived home, true to her word, Estelle told him all about Johanna and how she was at Higbee's Department Store riding the escalators, and that she'd been there for over two hours. After hearing the story and seeing his wife's angst, he put his hat and jacket back on and headed to Higbee's. A short time later, he returned with Johanna in tow.

Throwing off his jacket and placing his hat on the holder near the front door, he filled Estelle and Isabella in on the details while Johanna stood next to him, crestfallen.

"I walked into the store and sure enough, there she was—descending the escalator. I told her she only cared about herself and she is grounded for two weeks. Tonight, Estelle, she's to eat dinner then go straight to her room. That'll also be her routine when she returns from school in the week ahead."

He turned toward Johanna. "Now go eat your supper then go to your room."

"Yes, sir."

Johanna walked past Isabella, nudging and winking at her with a mischievous grin on her face. Isabella finally understood what the ornery look was for. Her older sister was brilliant. She had just "pulled a fast one" over on everyone because now she wouldn't have to clear or wash the dishes after dinner.

"Wait one minute!" Wanda shouted, her face turning red. "Why should Isabella and I be punished more than she will? She'll just go to her room and read while we do the dishes! That's not fair! Some punishment!"

Their father took a minute to think about it and then he shook his head. "Okay, I guess you're right. For now, Isabella will clear the dishes and you and Johanna will wash and dry them."

Wanda threw up her hands, declaring, "Ye, gads! She should do it all! But whatever."

When night arrived and Isabella pulled the bed covers to her chin while Johanna scrambled in as well, they both giggled about the day's events. "Jo Jo," Isabella asked her, a thought in her head that she'd been wanting to ask her sister for a long time. "Why do you disobey so often? Like why did you tell everyone a while back you'd have a birthday party, and why did you not come home with us tonight?"

There was a little silence as Johanna thought. Then she turned over on her back to face the ceiling, her brows drawn together. "Well, Izzy, I guess it's like this: We've gone through so many terrible times already that I want to make better things happen even if it means I get in trouble about it. When I saw the escalator, it seemed magical, and if

69

we're taken away again tomorrow and sent somewhere, when will I get the chance to ride those moving stairs again? See, something happened to me when Momma beat me, and I'm not scared any longer of people. I'm only scared if they hurt you. Does that make sense?"

Isabella nodded, thinking she did understand but knowing that she'd never have the bravery like Johanna to disobey adults. "I wish I was more like you, Jo Jo. You're the bravest person I know. I care too much about what Momma, Daddy, and Estelle think."

Johanna laughed, reaching under the covers to find and clasp Isabella's hand. "You do care too much about what they think, but you are brave too, Izzy. You stood up to that idiot, Junior, when he tried to get your clothes off and hurt Annie, and you rescued me a few times too."

Smiling, Isabella squeezed her hand. *Maybe she wasn't such a coward after all.*

"Sister, dear, bend near, so I can whisper my secret in your ear."

Giggling, Johanna leaned in. "What is it?"

"I heard Estelle telling Daddy earlier that she's taking us shopping tomorrow for decent school clothes. Won't that be exciting?"

"Oh yes!" Johanna squealed, hugging Isabella close. "It sure is. Now let's get some sleep so we look our best when we go."

Both girls fell quickly asleep.

They were warm, fed, and loved.

—⁊⟨⟨—

When the time drew near for the girls to go shopping for school clothes, they were each to buy three dresses. However, as they made their way through the aisles and gazed at the mannequins, Isabella fell in love with a blue checkered dress with matching hat. The more expensive dress prompted a warning from Estelle.

"Now, my dear," she said to Isabella. "If you are determined you want this particular dress, then you will only get two dresses. Do you understand?"

Isabella didn't care. She wanted that beautiful dress and was so happy when the clerk wrapped it in tissue paper then placed it inside a bag. She wore it as often as she could, and as Christmas approached during the months ahead, she decided she'd even wear it to church.

It didn't take long for the weather to turn cold and snowy. On Christmas Eve, a storm hit—creating a blanket of white all around. Isabella peered through their upstairs bedroom window, waiting on Johanna to finish brushing her teeth. The smell of cookies baking in the oven reached the upstairs rooms and Isabella's stomach growled.

How wonderful, she thought, *to experience such magic.*

She quickly grabbed Johanna's hand and pulled her downstairs where the first batch of cut-out cookies on a glass platter welcomed them. "We get to decorate them!" Johanna exclaimed, handing Isabella a cookie.

Estelle, a skilled cook, already had ham and turkey in the oven. Isabella was sure that not even heaven couldn't smell as good as the house at the moment. Even with four rowdy children on her hands, Estelle handled them well as she supervised their cookie-decorating tasks, saying she was so proud of them all.

The main event was the trimming of the Christmas tree. The tree lights were in a tangled heap, so the job of detangling them had been given to their father and David. Both Isabella and Johanna waited with baited breath to see if the lights worked, and clapped their hands ecstatically when the last strand was smoothed out and plugged in— every bulb lighting its brilliance for all to see. "Hooray!" cried Isabella. "We can now start hanging the beautiful Christmas bulbs." And shortly after, they did just that—each bulb unwrapped carefully, then hung with care with decorative icicles following next.

What a beautiful tree, Isabella thought. It was the most beautiful tree in the neighborhood. She stood still and admired the tree. And then the wonderful moment arrived where their father would place the angel on top of the tree. Stepping on the ladder, he teetered back and forth while attempting to place the angel on the tree's highest branch. Everyone stood wide-eyed and held their breath, but at last, shouts of glee erupted when he firmly positioned the angel in her place of honor and then leaned back, satisfied with his efforts.

Everyone talked at once about the beauty of the tree with its lights and angel. Isabella had been so excited about Christmas that she made Christmas cards and then carefully made or bought presents with her allowance for each member of the family. For Johanna, her gift was a green scarf to complement her green eyes and auburn hair, a blue scarf for Wanda to match her eyes, marbles for David, a rubber bathtub Ducky for Stella, cherry pipe tobacco for her father, and lastly, bubble bath for Estelle. She wanted to make certain Estelle was happy because she was such a kind stepmother who treated her and Johanna as her own daughters deserved to be.

Isabella sighed. Life was starting to be better than it ever had. She hoped it would stay that way.

CHAPTER NINE

*"I loved you too much to just be your friend. So God made
me your sister."*

"Would you mind if I called you Mother?" Isabella asked
Estelle during Christmas Eve. Obviously delighted, Estelle
reached down and pulled her into her arms.

"What a beautiful Christmas present you gave me, Isabella, by asking that question, and yes, you may!" She then kissed Isabella on the cheek.

"But now you must hurry and get ready for bed so that Santa can come," Estelle smiled. "Now hurry! Go to bed."

Isabella did just as she was told, eager for the morning to come, but her sister was reluctant to fall asleep. "Jo Jo, you *must* go to sleep or Santa won't come. I'm so tired from all the decorating and tree trimming, how could you not be tired?"

"I think it's all the cookies I ate!" Johanna laughed. "I'm overloaded with sugar."

Giggling, they talked until falling fast asleep. Shortly after, their father gently shook them awake. "What is it, Daddy? Is it Christmas morning already?" Isabella asked, rubbing her eyes.

Her father looked grim, his eyes narrowed as if something bad had happened. Isabella grew worried, nudging Johanna awake.

"No, Isabella," he finally answered, running his hand through his short, greying hair. "It's not Santa that has surprised us. I wish it was. We need you both to come downstairs."

Isabella and Johanna got out of bed, following his tall, narrow form, and walking down the stairs slowly while never letting go of each other's hands. When they all walked into the living room, they saw the reason for their father's grim countenance. Their mother and Howard were seated next to Estelle in a deep conversation. They all looked towards the archway when the girls walked in. Johanna let go of Isabella's hand and immediately Isabella put her hands behind her back, wringing them constantly—a terrible habit she'd begun a few years earlier when she'd become nervous.

Why is mother and Howard here? she thought. *And where is David and Wanda? Why aren't we opening our presents, and why is Mother crying?* Her heart raced, terrified at the unanswered questions in her mind.

"Girls," their father said to them, looking at each of their faces as if he were sorry for the next words he'd say. "Your mother has arrived here tonight to plead her case to take you both back to live with her."

"No!" Johanna blurted, "we want to stay here."

Their mother started crying harder. "I'm so alone, so alone. I miss you girls," Juliana said through sobs, prompting Howard to hand her a handkerchief.

"Please stop crying," their father told Juliana, shaking his head. "Let's talk about this reasonably without any drama."

Their mother didn't seem to like his comments as she sniffed a few times, wiped her nose, then sat up a bit straighter.

Isabella grew confused. She hated to see her mother cry, but she didn't want to go live with her, either. She turned to Johanna who stood perfectly still, her face expressionless. She wished Johanna would give her a signal on what to think.

"I know there were issues when they lived with me before, but I think those issues have been cleared up. Everyone has problems at first when they're adjusting to a new situation, but I miss having my daughters with me. I'm so lonely. Please come back to live with me."

The room grew silent, each in their own thoughts, and Isabella wondered how an evening so magical could turn so solemn within hours. Before Johanna and she had a chance to talk privately with one another, their father said, "Girls, you heard your mother and how she wants you to go back and live with her, but neither of you have to do that."

"Why don't you let the girls decide without your interference?" their mother said, standing up and then starting to cry again.

Elliott turned to each, and Isabella noticed how tired he looked. Or was he weary from whatever he and their mother had been discussing beforehand?

Estelle seemed disturbed too, and unusually quiet until she stood up to face Juliana. "I have an idea. Today has been a busy day and decisions like this shouldn't be made before a good night's rest. Can't we all just go to sleep and talk about this in the morning?"

Elliott shook his head. "Great idea, darling, but no." He swept his arm in a gesture that encompassed the room. "Look at this hard work, this magical night. I do not want to have problems on Christmas Day. Whatever we decide, we must decide tonight so that Christmas begins fresh."

He turned back to the girls, asking Johanna first if she wanted to live again with Juliana. Isabella squeezed Johanna's hand, tears falling softly to the floor as Johanna told him no. "I want to stay with you and Estelle."

Juliana gasped.

Elliott told her she could go to her room, and after she'd ascended the staircase, he looked toward Isabella. "Honey, look up at me."

Isabella lifted her chin, wishing that she was still clutching Johanna's hand. She looked from her father to her mother and then back again. Standing motionless, she thought about what was happening. Johanna would be with their father and Estelle, but who would be with their mother? Maybe her mother did have a change of heart and would be a better parent.

"I am so proud of you, Isabella," Juliana told her, breaking into her confusing thoughts. "All of your letters you sent me of your accomplishments made me so proud. They made me miss you girls so much. I am so lonely now, especially when Howard has to go far away for work."

"Please don't say things like that," Elliott told her. "Don't manipulate Isabella. She never sent you any letters."

"She did too!" Juliana defended, pulling out of her pocket several opened letters containing Isabella's grades.

Isabella blinked back tears. Her mother had read the letters but never responded. Why? And now the way her father looked at her, she felt as if she'd disappointed him by sneaking the letters in the mail.

"Little Isabella has always loved me," she said, sniffing. "Isn't that true, honey? And I'm so lonely without you."

Isabella's father turned back to her, repeating again that she didn't have to go live with her mother.

But somehow, Isabella already felt very sorry for her mother, and guilty that she'd have none of her children with her on Christmas Day. Maybe she truly did have a change of heart.

Estelle and Elliott had Johanna, David, Wanda, and Stella. If she decided to stay with Estelle and her father, Juliana would have no children.

"I will go stay with Momma," Isabella said, and even though the words came out as a whisper, it was as if she had shouted them. Their mother clapped her hands, rushing over to her and hugging her tightly.

Estelle gasped, and Elliott asked Isabella if she was certain of her answer. She shook her head yes. Her mother's arms felt wonderful around her—something she'd wanted her whole life. It truly felt as if her mother now loved her.

"Then go upstairs and pack your belongings," he told her, and Isabella knew that somehow she had disappointed him in a very deep way. "You may take all the Christmas gifts your mother and Howard brought here for you tonight, but you cannot take your gifts from us. Those gifts stay here, since they were intended for you to play with here."

"Yes, Father." And that was all Isabella could manage to say. Tears welled up in her eyes as she swallowed hard. Not only had she disappointed her father and Estelle, but she would be separated from Johanna as well. *How can I ever survive being away from her?* After all, she and Johanna were so close, it was if when Johanna breathed, Isabella exhaled.

And how will I be able to tell Johanna that I'm leaving?

Despaired, she wrung her hands, heading upstairs as her father reminded her again to gather her belongings. Opening the bedroom door, she noticed Johanna was tucked in bed when she entered the room but still somewhat awake. Isabella thought it would've been easier to not tell her the news if she had been asleep. Instead, Johanna rolled over and asked, "Well? Can you believe Momma wanted us to go live with her?"

Isabella shrugged and didn't answer, but instead, rummaged quietly around the room as to not draw attention to the fact that she was packing. Gathering her stuffed dog, Rags, she then shoved her clothes in a bag.

"What are you doing? Please tell me you didn't say yes!" Johanna exclaimed, jumping from bed and then she burst into tears. "You did, didn't you? Oh, Izzy, how could you? How could you say you'll go back to her and them and Junior? Why would you leave me? Why....?"

The tears that Isabella had held back now burst forth. Sobbing, she sank to the floor. "I'm so sorry, so sorry, but Momma looked so sad, and I kept thinking of all of us here and that she had no one."

"She deserves to have no one," Johanna said through sobs. "Oh my God, Isabella! You're so foolish! Do you realize what you've done? You always wanted her approval and now you made a mistake! I can't protect you there! Don't you see that? And now, you've gone and separated us. You are my heart, Izzy, and I don't know how it can beat without you every day."

Johanna was more upset than Isabella had ever seen her. She put her head in her hands and cried. "Oh, Johanna! I'm so sorry! I feel the same way about you, but we can visit, can't we? Or I can come back again. Right? I just didn't want Momma to cry anymore. She seems like she loves us now."

Johanna grabbed a few tissues from the nightstand, handing one to Isabella. After blowing her nose and wiping her tears from her cheeks, Johanna whispered, "Don't you understand, little Izzy, that if she truly loved you she wouldn't be asking you or us to come back and live with her? If she truly loved us, she'd want us to be here, somewhere safe and happy. And she wouldn't have done this on Christmas Eve!"

Their father called to them, telling Isabella to hurry. Both girls walked to the top of the staircase and looked down. Johanna grabbed Isabella's hand and brought it to her chest. "Please, Isabella, please don't go. Stay with me."

Juliana shouted up to Isabella now too, appearing at the bottom of the stairs and motioning for her to hurry down. Isabella jumped forward in surprise at her mother's loud voice and the hold she had on Johanna's hand broke apart. Both girls gazed down at their hands, which now were individually placed by their sides, as if just realizing after all these years that they were two people and not one. Sadness cloaked itself around them as Isabella stifled more tears and began walking down the steps, but she could hear Johanna's angry voice behind her.

"Grandmother Swain was right about you! You *are* dumb!" Johanna shouted.

Her sister's words couldn't have hurt worse if they'd been a knife.

When she reached the bottom of the stairs, she turned, looked upward, but Johanna had already stormed into her bedroom. Isabella lowered her head, then lifted it and blew a kiss like they'd done in the past to each other. It would be the last kiss she gave her for a long time, for life would never be the same again. Her beloved Johanna would not be with her.

CHAPTER TEN

"I can't promise to solve all your problems, but I can promise you won't have to face them alone."

"Howard, how much longer is it until we get home?" asked Isabella, knowing that the word "home" had never sounded so empty, for many she loved were miles away.

"We are just about there," he answered.

Her tired eyes closed and within minutes she was asleep until bump in the road caused her to awaken and shout out for Johanna.

"Isabella, wake up! Wake up. Johanna is not here," her mother said, nudging her with her hand. "She stayed with your father, remember?"

"Oh, I remember now," Isabella whispered, tears forming in her eyes.

"Now, none of that," Howard said, glancing at her in the rearview mirror. "No crying. It's almost Christmas morning, and looky here, we just arrived home."

He pulled the car into the driveway.

Isabella sat up fully and looked around outside, trying to remember what her former home looked like.

Nowhere was the life present of the home she'd just left behind. Instead, it was dark and dismal with Grandmother Swain's foreboding house right next to it. Isabella swallowed hard, following her mother and Howard out of the car and into the house. She clutched her stuffed dog to her, hoping that Junior was nowhere around.

"Now it's my turn to get the Christmas tree looking beautiful," Juliana announced, hurrying around to gather a few ornaments and tinsel. After trimming the tree, she then placed a few Christmas presents under it so that Isabella would have a few gifts to open in the morning.

Isabella wondered at the positive change in her mother. Could it be she truly loved her? The thought filled Isabella with hope that maybe her decision to leave with her mother had been the right one. But she also knew that Johanna had been right, too. That she had always, for whatever reason, wanted the approval of her mother in all things. But still, now that she was here with her, and her mother was acting loving, it couldn't replace the fresh emptiness of not having Johanna beside her.

After Howard and her mother told her to go to bed, she laid back on the familiar couch she had left a few months ago, the one that was worn, dingy and damp and she missed the comforts she'd had at her father's house.

Hugging Rags to her, she wondered how Annie would be doing at her father's house. Surely they would take good care of her cat. She had never asked her mother if she could bring Annie back to stay with them because she knew that if Junior was still around, which he most likely would be, then Annie would be in danger.

She knew it would be Christmas morning soon, but somehow, nothing seemed as magical without Johanna holding her hand. With tears in her eyes, she prayed that sleep would come quickly.

Hours later, and with a gentle display of snowflakes swirling outside the house's windows, Isabella awoke. She stretched, yawned, and rolled on her side, noticing that her mother had turned on the lights on in the Christmas tree and they sparkled beautifully.

"Good morning," her mother said from the kitchen, walking into the living room with a cup of coffee in her hand. "Well, sleepyhead, are you going to open your gifts?"

For a moment, thoughts of sadness evaporated like stray raindrops on hot desert sand. Isabella bolted from the couch and ran to the tree, grabbing the gifts her mother pointed to.

Opening each present, she smiled. It felt so good to know her mother had thought of her, and her mother seemed truly happy that she had one of her daughters with her on Christmas morning. *Maybe I did make the right decision in coming back after all,* Isabella thought.

When all her presents were opened, she placed the items in a neat row in front of her. She'd received a baton, a Dictionary, and a few pairs of new underwear. Twirling the baton through her fingers, she tried to get the knack of twirling it faster, but her mother told her they must get dressed for Grandmother Swain's house to share Christmas breakfast with them.

Instantly, Isabella's smile disappeared.

"Now, don't look so worried," Howard said as he entered the room and noticed her frown. "I'll be there too, and things have changed since you've been gone."

Isabella was still uncertain as to what happened to create such positive changes in her mother's behavior, or for that matter, even Grandmother Swain's if what Howard said was true. However, she knew she'd find out quickly enough and so she prepared herself, washing her face, and changing into clothes from her bag that she'd brought back from her father's.

When they walked next door to her grandmother's, Junior's voice could be heard before they even entered the front door. Instantly, Isabella's stomach tightened and nausea set in. She stopped a moment until her mother tugged her arm, then paused and looked at her.

No, no, no! Isabella said to herself, not wanting to enter the house.

Juliana looked down at her, her arched eyebrows drawn together. "What's the matter with you?" she asked. "Are you not feeling well? Is it a sore throat? You keep swallowing hard."

Isabella wondered if she should tell her mother the real reason she looked ill. She then decided against it. She hadn't been around her mother long enough to know if her mother had truly changed or if she'd somehow punish her for speaking the truth.

"I don't feel well, Momma," she told her. "My throat is hurting some."

"Well, that throws a lot of concerns in the mix," her mother said, looking disappointed. "Go on home and rest. We can't have you getting anyone else sick."

Isabella nodded, hurrying back to her house and feeling like she had just dodged a bullet.

The following weeks proved that not really much had changed in the lives of those around her, including her own. She still had to use the smelly outhouse, and it gagged her so badly that sometimes she found herself longing to disappear in the back woods for a moment to take care of her needs. But she knew that if Junior spied her, he would follow and harm her.

School was uneventful, her grades a little above average to try and please her mother, and for whatever unknown reasons her mother wanted her daughters back, her nurturing desire when she got Isabella home quickly dimmed. Although her mother's behavior didn't change as quickly as she remembered from kind to mean to brooding, Juliana was still moody, and her new job meant working the afternoon shifts. So during the school day, her mother was asleep, and when Isabella returned home, her mother was at work. Even Howard worked away so often that the house was usually empty, and Isabella found herself alone, constantly worried about Junior trying to sneak in, and always at every second of every day, she'd think of her beloved sister that she had left behind.

When the school year started the next semester, Isabella was in the sixth-grade and Johanna was in the eighth-grade back with her father. For the first few weeks of Isabella's school, Juliana had forbidden her to wash her hair at home or in the creek. Isabella hadn't known the reasons, but her mother had been acting differently, and Howard had explained that the cause might've been new medication she was on. Whatever the reason for the mood swings, Isabella could find no valid reason why she wasn't allowed to wash her hair.

One day at school, her class was called to the gym locker room to have their heads checked for lice. The teacher passed by Isabella, stopped, and pinched her nose. "Isabella, I have never seen a filthier head of hair or scalp in all my years of teaching. I'm certain you have lice."

Embarrassed, Isabella prayed silently and was so thankful when the school nurse examined her and then said she didn't show signs of lice. But her relief didn't last long.

"When is the last time your hair was washed?" one of the nurses said. "It's absolutely horrible! You go home today and tell your parents you need to be properly bathed and your hair washed too, do you understand?"

"Yes, Ma'am," Isabella whispered, mortified.

A few minutes later when she walked back into the classroom, most of her classmates were already seated. They all pointed at her. "Heyyyy Cootie Girl, go back home! Ewww! You stink!"

Isabella slunk down, wishing she were an ant and could disappear through a crack. She took her seat until lunch was signaled. If she thought her classmates had forgotten her and her hair, she was wrong. They laughed, mocked, and ran away from her until she ran from them and hid herself behind the building until the school bell rang to announce that recess was over.

The rest of the school day was brutal, and when over, she hurried to the school bus, so thankful to be going home.

When she busted through the door to her house a short time later, her mother reprimanded her high energy until she saw the tears on her face.

"What happened?" her mother asked, and Isabella broke down, crying.

"Why wouldn't you allow me to wash my hair? You and Grandmother Swain did that years ago to me! The kids all made fun of me. The teacher said I smell! The nurse said you must wash my hair, Momma!"

Instead of the hug and apology she hoped to receive from her mother, she instead, received a head-washing in the kitchen sink. "Who the hell do they think they are telling me what I must do with my own children?" she mumbled to Isabella while scrubbing her head.

And that's what Isabella would remember the rest of her life. No explanation, no reasoning for sending her to school for so long without proper bathing. No apology.

The school year progressed in an awful fashion for Isabella from then on, and when she returned home, although she didn't mind sleeping on the couch, she hated how many times Junior would try to get inside her home. On one frightful night when she was alone, the front doorknob rattled. At first it was a slow jiggling sound, but then became furiously loud. Isabella had quickly gone into the kitchen, looking for a weapon, ready to use it on Junior if he busted in.

One time she hid behind the couch, her heart racing with fear as he didn't stop rattling the handle and almost seemed to be trying to pick the lock. Isabella had thought for sure that would be the time he'd get in, but out in the distance a female voice rang out.

"Junior? Where are you? You better get your behind in this house! Dinner is ready!"

Isabella recognized that the voice belonged to her Aunt Priscilla, and let out a huge sigh of relief.

"Okay, Mom, I'm coming!" he hollered back, and his annoyed voice sent a shiver up Isabella's spine.

Isabella stayed behind the couch until it was safe to come out. How she hated times like these where living with her mother and Howard seemed never-ending. She often thought of what Johanna would tell her at those times of anxiety, and she knew that although her sister was disappointed that she had decided to live with their mother, Johanna would still have enough love in her beautiful heart to forgive her and want her safe and happy. She knew that Johanna would tell her to hold onto hope and that once she graduated high school, she could get a job and move away from the little dark house by Grandmother Swain's.

That time seems so far away, Isabella thought, wondering how she'd get through so many school years without Johanna. *Church,* she thought, *I'll just concentrate on church.* Out of all her days living with her mother and Howard, Sunday was her happiest. She would walk the mile to the clapboard white church on the hill, its steeple a beacon to her of hope and love, and she'd collect pennies throughout the week she'd earned for chores or if she'd find any on the road, and she'd place all but one in the collection plate. The one penny she'd keep was to buy a pretzel at the church to eat on her journey home.

Although she loved the new church, she also missed the one she'd attended when she lived with her father. That church allowed one child from each Sunday service to ring the bell to announce that church had ended. Oh, how she loved to ring the church bell when it was her turn. She'd grasp the long rope and pull as hard as she could to make the bells ring. Just hearing the melodic gonging filled her with a sense of excitement.

Maybe one day I'll get back to that church, she thought, remembering their Bible summer school and how she and Johanna had looked forward to it. Everyone at that church had been so nice.

During the days after school, Isabella loved to listen to the radio program called the Living Bible and especially the Bible story of Ruth. Maybe she loved that particular story so much because Ruth went through tough times yet later received tremendous blessings.

Whatever the reasons, Isabella knew that the Bible was one of her favorite things in life and everyone knew it. Even her classmates who were required to read a Bible verse each day knew it. When one student would be too shy to read a verse out loud, Isabella was always the first to volunteer to read it for that student.

"Isabella, what is it about the Bible that you love so much?" her teacher had asked her one day in front of the other students.

"It brings me comfort and happiness," she had replied, and the teacher seemed to like that answer very much as she smiled and hugged her.

That hug had meant the world to her. After all, maybe, just maybe those at the school were forgetting about her "cooties."

Those special moments when someone was kind to her helped Isabella also with her environment with her mother. She'd never forget when she arrived home from school one day and her mother told her to get into their truck.

"Where are we going?" she had asked her.

"To Mr. Walling's to get that money he owes me for a cow I sold him."

"The cow you kept in back of our house and raised for beef?"

"What other cow would it be, Isabella? Don't be stupid."

Maybe it was a stupid question, and Isabella figured she certainly asked a lot of them because someone always seemed to be pointing out that fact.

"Are you sure you want to go there, Momma?" she asked her. "I thought you said a few days ago that there would be trouble when you saw Mr. Walling."

"We're going whether there's trouble or not," her mother replied, and so they left and headed to Mr. Walling's home. The winding road to his house was beautiful. Green pastures lie all around with sheep dotting the hillsides, reminding Isabella of the picturesque paintings she'd seen in the school library.

When twenty more minutes or so passed, Mr. Walling's house loomed magnificently in the distance—a high, ornate gate positioned in front of his driveway seemed placed there as if announce Mr. Walling's wealth.

Isabella's mother parked the truck as close as she could to the gate, honked the horn several times, then got out of the truck and started yelling, "I want my money, you dirty bastard! You better get out here, Walling, and give me my money or I'm going to drive this truck through these fine gates of yours!" She got back into the truck, holding onto the brake while revving the engine threateningly.

Within minutes, Walling appeared on the opposite side of the gate with a rifle.

"What the hell are you talking about, woman?" he shouted back to Juliana. "I have the bill of sale right here." He reached his free hand into his pocket and withdrew a white piece of paper. "Paid in Full, it says. Signed by me and you! Now if you don't get out of here this minute, I'm calling the Sheriff and I'll have you arrested for trespassing!"

Isabella watched from the passenger side of the truck as her mother stuck her head out of the window. "Why, you dirty low-life liar! You know damn well you told me you forgot the money in your other pants after I signed that! I trusted you to get the money and come right back. Well, it's no wonder you're so rich. You are a thief and liar!"

"Get outta here! Now!"

"Oh, I'm going!" Juliana shouted, slamming the truck into reverse.

"But I hope you die with your guts on fire, and I wouldn't piss on you to help put it out."

"Get going!" he shouted. "And take your gawky-eyed brat with you before I do away with both of you!"

"All right, you mealy-mouthed bastard, but someday you'll lose all of your wealth and you'll be nothing more than a cow turd! And I'll be there to laugh at you."

Juliana accelerated the truck, using a maneuver Isabella had seen her do only one other time while driving, and it sent gravel and dirt flying everywhere from under the rear tires.

When Isabella turned back in her seat to look out of the rear window, she saw Mr. Walling coughing in a dust cloud of debris. She gazed at her mother, noticing the satisfied smirk on her face. Although Mr. Walling most likely had that little revenge coming, Isabella couldn't shake the feeling of how angry her mother could get. Like how she beat Johanna and now how her anger spilled over to Mr. Walling.

Swallowing hard, she turned back to the front window and stared ahead, hoping she never made her mother mad.

CHAPTER ELEVEN

"Sisters by chance. Friends by choice."

The next school day began as usual, but when Isabella returned from it and to her home, she froze when she entered the front door. Everything was gone. No furniture, none of her clothes, no kitchen table, nothing! *They abandoned her! They must have!*

Nauseous, she sunk to the floor, sobbing. *Why would they do that to her and what would she do now?*

Wringing her hands, she uttered a prayer and then heard the sounds of a vehicle approaching. Standing and running towards the door, she breathed a sigh of relief. The rattley old Ford truck was coming up the hill. She ran outside on the porch and clung to her mother as she stepped out.

"What in the world is the matter with you?" Juliana said, pushing her away slightly to look her in the eyes. "Have you gone daft, Izzy?"

"I thought you all left me! Where's the furniture and everything?"

Juliana made a clicking throat noise as if disapproving of Isabella's assumption. "We wouldn't do that! There are insects in the house and we moved everything to clean. The furniture is out back." She peeled Isabella's arms from her waist. "Now go on and get back in the house. If you have homework, do it now because I'll need you when we move the furniture back in shortly."

"I don't have any homework, Momma," Isabella said, wondering why her mother looked pale and upset.

"Then go over to Grandmother's house and start bringing some of the boxes of clothes back to our house."

Isabella froze. It had been so long since she'd been around Junior, she was beginning to hope she'd never see him again.

"Go on," her mother said, nudging her. She must've picked up on her fright as she added, "Junior has a new toy gun that shoots real darts. He has a target out back. He'll probably let you shoot the gun."

"I don't care about a toy gun," Isabella said, wanting to run away and hide instead of go to Grandmother Swain's house. "They are mean to me, Momma, and they lie. I don't want to go without you!"

"They are our family, Isabella, and they might annoy us sometimes but they have not lied that I know about nor have they hurt you. Now, do as I say, and GO."

Isabella jumped at her mother's raised voice, then she started walking toward her grandmother's house. Behind her she could hear her mother telling Howard that her head was still hurting.

"I think it's a migraine," he told her, and Juliana agreed. "When you get in there, darling, and the furniture is moved, make certain you rest."

Isabella knocked on Grandmother Swain's door and Junior opened it with his hands holding the dart gun she'd just heard about.

"What do you want, you stupid brat?" he asked, his beady eyes zeroing in on her as if she were a tasty strip of meat. "Don't think I'm going to let you play with my new gun."

"I'm here to carry our boxes back to the house," Isabella told him, crossing over the threshold and into the house. "I don't want to play with your gun."

Just then, the familiar and eerie clucking sound of rubber hitting the floorboards could be heard. Grandmother Swain appeared around the corner of the kitchen, her cane rapping on the floorboards.

"Well, well, well," she said, looking over Isabella. "If it isn't the golden child—blonde hair, blue eyes, and evil."

"I am not evil," Isabella defended, not liking that word, especially since the Bible talked about it. "I'm here to get boxes."

"You're not here to ask Junior to play with his new gun?"

Isabella grew even more uncomfortable, wishing that her mother or Howard would appear. "No, Ma'am. I don't want to play with his gun."

"Of course you want to play with his new gun because you're selfish and jealous that he has something new."

Isabella didn't reply. Instead, she moved slightly away from the wall she'd been pressed up against and then looked around the room, spotting a few boxes with familiar items. "I'll just grab one of these boxes and be on my way."

She hurried to one of the boxes, hoisted it up, and struggled with its weight to carry it next door, but she refused to drop it. She wanted out of Grandmother Swain's house as quickly as possible.

When she'd gotten the box into her own home, she quickly placed it on the floor, then rubbed her aching hands.

"She did not!" a voice that Isabella recognized as her mother's rang out somewhere outside. "Isabella would not do that."

"Oh, no…" Isabella whispered, her stomach tightening at what disaster could be happening outside.

"Isabella? Isabella, if you hear me, come outside," her mother called.

Isabella reluctantly walked outside and down the steps to her mother who was standing in the yard with Grandmother Swain. "Yes, Momma?"

Juliana looked down at her, and then nodded her head toward where Junior stood on the front porch. "Did you take Junior's gun and lose it?" she asked her.

92

"Of course not, Momma!" Isabella exclaimed, shaking her head vigorously. "He had it with him, but I never touched it! I swear!"

Juliana's brows drew together as if her headache had just worsened. She studied Isabella's face for a moment and then turned to Grandmother Swain. "She's telling the truth," she said. "She didn't touch it."

Thrilled and hugely relieved that her mother believed her, she let out the breath she'd been holding until Grandmother Swain spoke. "She most certainly touched it. I saw her with my very own eyes! She was playing with it in the back yard before she took that box back!"

"I did not!" Isabella shouted, and then tears stung her eyes and she started to cry.

Grandmother Swain lifted her hand as if she were going to slap her. "Then you must be calling me a liar, you little snot!"

"Listen," Juliana said, turning to the older woman whose mouth was contorted in an angry line. "Isabella said she didn't touch it and you're saying you saw her. This makes no sense."

"So you're calling me a liar now too?" Grandmother Swain asked Juliana. "Who is the adult here between me and this brat? And you're taking a child's word for it? I saw her hold that gun in her hand while Junior wasn't around, and now, it's missing! And you're going to believe her when both Junior and I know she had it?" She pointed to the house. "Go inside and outside and look around. You won't find it anywhere 'cause only your brat knows where she put it."

Juliana took up the challenge, disappearing in the house and then searching the outside yard before returning. "Okay, I'm baffled like you, but it doesn't mean that Isabella took, lost, or hid it."

Just then, Junior's voice rang out, "I want my gun! She took it because she was jealous!" And then he started to cry.

"What in the world would you like me to do? I can't perform magic and have that gun appear!" Juliana exclaimed.

"I think you know what to do," Grandmother Swain told Juliana, her eyes narrowing on Isabella. "Beat the answer out of her! You must beat that child for this. She's a liar and a thief and now she and you are calling me a liar! Let me get a belt strap and punish her for such evil!'

Juliana put a hand on Grandmother Swain's arm as she raised it toward Isabella. "I'll take care of it," she told her. "I'll punish her."

"No!" Isabella pleaded, throwing her arms around her mother's waist and sobbing. "I didn't do anything wrong. Please, Momma, please!"

"Come back into the house with me, Izzy," her mother said, tugging her along toward the house. "Grandmother Swain is the adult and she said she saw you so you must be lying. Now, you'll be punished."

Sobbing harder, Isabella turned slightly to notice that Junior had stopped crying, and also, that her grandmother was smirking.

Once inside the house, Juliana told Isabella to wait for her in the kitchen while she got a belt to whip her with. She returned a few minutes later with one of Howard's leather belts.

"Momma, please," Isabella cried, "I didn't do anything! I'm not lying."

Juliana put her fingers to her mouth to signal to her to be quiet. As hard as it was, Isabella sniffed a few times then quieted. Her mother leaned down and whispered, "I'm going to hit the table with the belt. Every time I do, I want you to scream. You understand?"

Relieved, Isabella almost fainted against her mother. "Yes," she nodded, and then her mother proceeded to hit the table hard with the belt strap. Each time she did, Isabella screamed and cried until her mother told her to stop.

She then signaled for Isabella to follow her. They went to the front door, and peeked around the corner to see both Grandmother Swain and Junior on the front porch, smiling as if they won the lottery. No doubt their joy was at Isabella's supposed beating. They both then went back into their house, but a few minutes later, Grandmother Swain returned to the front porch, looked around, and then quickly reached up to the porch roof rafters and retrieved Junior's toy gun.

"That bitch," Juliana whispered, and then turned to Isabella. "I had a feeling you were being set up."

Isabella swallowed hard, so relieved to be free from suspicion and punishment, but at the same time, so frightened and hurt that Grandmother Swain would do something like this to get her punished. *Why does she hate me so much?*

As if her mother read her thoughts, she told her, "Isabella, Grandmother Swain has a bitter soul. She is jealous of you for whatever reasons, and I started to see it a while ago but didn't want to believe she was lying. But tonight I realized the hard truth. Don't be scared of her anymore."

Even though her mother told her that, they were only words. Isabella knew that she should always be frightened of Grandmother Swain and Junior. No matter how many years passed.

When Howard returned later from work that evening, Isabella could hear her mother talking with him.

"You know, Howard, your mother is a vicious woman. I just found out what she did so that Izzy would be punished."

"I can't believe she would do anything like that," he said.

"Well, she did, and I hear from the neighbors that she is planning on moving away soon. That'll be the best for everyone. Is that true?"

"Well, she is moving to Willsville, Pennsylvania, for a while to care for an older relative," he told her, setting his jacket and hat on the kitchen chair. "It was confirmed today." He looked at Isabella then back at Juliana. "So Izzy won't have to be around her any longer."

"I don't think that's good enough," Juliana said. "Do you realize how many times I punished Izzy in the past based on what your mother told me?"

He sighed. "Well, what do you propose I do now, Juliana? I can't go back in time to fix it. And I'm hoping you don't expect me to confront her about it. Everything will work out just fine." He put his hands on her shoulders. "I had an idea earlier. I was wondering if your sister, Lottie, would like to rent my mother's house. Just think of that possibility! If she did rent it, you'd have your sister and her children right next door to you."

"Where's Junior and Priscilla going to live? Are they going with your mother?"

"No," he told her. "They are moving and renting the house right next door to the one your sister will be in. Our families will be in all three houses right in a row. Won't that be wonderful?"

Isabella could think of many other things that would be wonderful but not that scenario. Still, though, even if Junior stayed behind with his mother, she'd be thankful at least that Grandmother Swain would be gone.

A week later, on a rainy Saturday morning, Isabella awoke to men's voices and clanking sounds. Rushing from the couch to the front door, she squealed in delight. There was Grandmother Swain with movers helping her load her belongings into the back of a truck.

Thank you, God! After all this time, her prayers were finally being answered.

Just like Howard had said, Junior and his mother moved to the house next to Grandmother Swain's old house, and Aunt Lottie, her husband, Finn, and their children, Sergei, Cole, Edwin, and Whitney moved into Grandmother Swain's house.

"Isn't this wonderful," Isabella's mother told her the next day. "Your favorite cousins are now living right next door to us."

Isabella didn't know what to think yet of her cousins. They seemed nice enough, but Whitney and Cole moved out soon for college, which left only Edwin and Sergei who were close in age, only a year apart. They seemed to have a great brotherly bond, as Edwin would often tell Sergei to mind his elders, meaning that Sergei was to respect him as one. Sergei would just laugh, and then they'd be off running around the neighborhood. Isabella liked the favorable stories she'd hear about them from other children. Even the teachers told her that Edwin and Sergei were well-liked and that Sergei was already earning the reputation of a peacemaker.

Life would've been better than it had been if it wasn't for one significant problem. Junior. He was still the meanest boy in town and still causing problems. One day, he caught a snake and chased anyone he could find with it—targeting Isabella the most because she hated snakes. Terrified, she ran away but he soon caught up to her. That is, until Edwin and Sergei pushed him away and grabbed the snake, throwing it over the hill.

Junior had stomped angrily into his house, and then the next day exacted his revenge. With a bagful of jagged rocks, he began throwing them with all his might at Isabella as she returned from school. One of the rocks hit the corner of her eye, piercing her skin and opening a floodgate of blood.

Juliana, hearing the screams, ran out of the house and toward Isabella. Sergei and Edwin were shouting what had happened and Juliana turned toward Junior, cursing him. "What is the matter with you, you filthy rotten brat! You always have to hurt someone to make yourself feel important, don't you?"

Holding the palm of her hand against Isabella's eye to stop the bleeding, she helped her toward their house while Junior walked away—his cocky strides showing how unaffected he was by Juliana's rage.

A moment before he climbed the porch steps to his house, Sergei and Edwin grabbed a handful of rocks, picked a few heavy smooth ones and zinged them at Junior—hitting him in the back of the head.

Screaming, he lifted his hands to his head and shouted for his mother. She ran out of the front door and down the steps.

"What happened?" she shouted, putting her arms around him. "Who did this to you?"

Junior rubbed the back of his head, tears streaming down his pudgy cheeks as he pointed toward Isabella.

"I did not!" she yelled to them, clinging to her mother's waist. "He hit me with a rock!"

She peeked around her mother's back to notice two figures dashing toward a tree. It was Edwin and Sergei. They winked at her before they disappeared in the bushes lining the driveways.

"Juliana, you better get those kids under control or I'm going to call the sheriff and have them arrested," said Priscilla.

"Go ahead, Priscilla, call them and while they are here, I'll show them what Junior did to Izzy's eye." She moved Izzy toward the front of their house, shouting, "You are raising the devil himself! There is never any trouble unless your evil boy is around!"

"It's your daughters!" Priscilla shouted back. "They are trouble-makers, and if you are such a great mother, why did your oldest brat not want to live with you?"

Isabella felt her mother's hand tighten on hers and knew that she was close to exploding her temper on Priscilla just like she had with Mr. Walling.

"Momma, can we just go inside and get something for my eye? It hurts," Isabella told her, and she wasn't lying to just try and save her mother from more of a fight with Junior's mom. Nope. Her eye did hurt, and she hoped it would get better real soon.

Juliana gazed down at Isabella, and then cursed a few times at Priscilla as they made their way into the house. Once inside, her mother grabbed a sponge, soaking it in cool water, wringing it, then dabbing it on Isabella's eye.

Once Isabella's eye was taken care if with a little soap and water, a truck door could be heard slamming outside their house. A few seconds later, Howard came inside asking Juliana what had happened. The temper that her mother had held in check now exploded on him. Shaking, Isabella walked quietly into the living room and sat on the couch while they yelled about Priscilla and Junior.

"Look, I'm sorry you're going through this, but it's over now. Why don't we all just get into the truck and go to that new ice cream shop up the road? You can even ask your nephews and Lottie to come."

That invitation seemed to appease Juliana, and after a few minutes, she stopped frowning and left the house to return a short time later with Sergei and Edwin in tow.

"They're going to come, but Lottie has a headache and is staying in."

Even though her eye was still hurting, just seeing Sergei and Edwin and knowing they were all about to enjoy ice cream made the pain better.

"Okay, everyone, get in the truck," Howard said, and everyone did just as he said, scrambling for the front door. Edwin, Sergei, and Isabella rode in the back of the truck and they laughed all the way to the store.

"Did you hear that big thud when I threw the rock and it hit his head?" Sergei asked Edwin.

"I sure did!" Edwin laughed, and Isabella joined in. How wonderful it felt to have others stick up for her against Junior, just like Johanna used to do.

Isabella's smile dimmed.

"Hey, no sad faces," Edwin said, patting her knee. "Whatcha thinkin' of?"

"My sister," Isabella answered, feeling as though an eternity had passed since she last saw her. "I miss her."

"We'd love to meet her again," Edwin said, his kind eyes narrowing as he tried figuring out the math on how long it had been since they'd seen her. "I think it was three years ago. I'm not sure, but maybe one day we can all visit your father and her."

"Oh, I hope so!" Isabella shouted, hugging Edwin as the truck neared the ice cream shop. It came to a complete stop, and then Howard shifted into park and stepped outside the vehicle. "Okay, everyone, jump out and head inside."

Excitedly all three children did just that, and Isabella told herself to mark that day down in her mind because it was a good day. When they all returned home, Isabella stepped inside the house first and noticed an envelope that the postal worker had slipped under the front door.

"What is that?" she asked, pointing to the letter.

"Must be the child-support check from your father," Howard replied.

Confused, Isabella looked at her mother. "Daddy pays you for me to be here?"

Juliana looked upset, throwing Howard an angry look, then she turned back to Isabella. "Yes, your father pays me for the added expenses of having you here, but it is not enough."

Even though the evening had been wonderful with Sergei and Edwin and enjoying ice cream, Isabella felt sad that the whole time she'd been with her mother she'd thought that her mom wanted her there just because she loved her. Now, somehow, she began to realize that maybe the whole reason her mother wanted her there was to receive money from her father.

"That doesn't look like the same envelope you usually receive," Howard said, and then Juliana walked over to it, stooped down and picked it up.

"Well, it's addressed to me," she said, "and looks like Elliott's sloppy handwriting, so let's see." She tore off part of the envelope and slipped the letter out then began to read. "Yes! Yes! Yes!" she exclaimed, shaking her head and seeming very satisfied at what the letter said. "This is unbelievable!" Turning to Isabella, she said, "Your father and Estelle are getting a divorce! He writes that with his current job and the traveling that he won't be able to care for Johanna properly. He said that even though she's upset, he is forcing her to come live with us."

"Johanna is coming to live with us?" Isabella practically squealed. "For sure? I'm so sorry that father and Estelle are getting a divorce but Johanna gets to come stay with us now! I'm so happy!"

"So am I," Juliana whispered to Howard and winked. "That's twice the check."

"When will she come here?" Isabella asked, clapping her hands.

"Tomorrow we will pick her up," Juliana informed her, reading the rest of the letter. "It's a four-hour drive, so if you are going with us, be up and ready because we're leaving at 7:00 am."

That night, Isabella couldn't fall asleep. Oh, how she missed her beautiful sister and the secrets they would share. They'd always been there for one another, and life hadn't been the same since separated. Now, Johanna would be back and they could begin their secrets once again by saying to each other: "Sister, dear, bend near, so I can whisper my secret in your ear."

The next morning didn't dawn quickly enough for Isabella. After a night of tossing and turning, she rushed off of the couch, dressed quickly, and waited on the front porch stoop for her mother and Howard. An hour later, they were all nestled inside the truck, and Isabella felt as if she could count every mile to her beloved Johanna. When they finally arrived at their destination, Howard hadn't even shifted the truck into park before Isabella crawled over her mother, was out the door, and running towards the house.

Before she stepped onto the front porch, the house door opened and Johanna came barreling down to Isabella, throwing her arms around her. Both of them just spun around, laughing and hugging one another.

"I've missed you so much!" Johanna said, breathless as she stopped twirling to push herself back from Isabella to study her. "Well, you've grown taller, that's for sure. And your cheeks aren't so full."

Isabella didn't want to tell her that was mostly due to there not being much food in the house. Life hadn't been as bad as when she and Johanna both lived with her mother, but there were still times of barely a crumb in the kitchen.

The front door opening again brought both their attention to the house. Wanda, David, and little Stella, who was now walking and not an infant any longer, appeared. Their father stood behind them, but Estelle wasn't there. After everyone greeted one another warmly, Isabella turned to Johanna. "Where is Estelle?"

Johanna's green eyes turned serious. She leaned in to Isabella. "Sister, dear, bend near, so I can whisper my secret in your ear."

Isabella knew that what she might tell her was something very somber, but for now, she loved having her sister say those words again. Once she leaned in, Johanna whispered, "I heard Daddy and Estelle fighting. Daddy accused her of being a closet alcoholic."

Isabella cupped her hand over her mouth so not to shout her surprise. Estelle? An alcoholic? That couldn't be true! Estelle was so nice and seemed like she'd never do something like that.

"I couldn't believe it at first either," Johanna said low, "but then I started to see her drinking a lot at night, and then Daddy and her started arguing. I heard Daddy say that she drank at first to ease her headaches and back pain and then it had gotten worse."

Isabella shook her head. She loved Estelle so much. It saddened her to think she might not see her again, but she had beautiful Johanna back and so life was still brighter.

She chit-chatted with Wanda and David, and then her father appeared outside with Johanna's suitcases. Isabella glimpsed her cat,

Annie, in the doorway and was able to love on her before Howard said they should be leaving.

Hugging her father, Isabella turned her head upwards for his kiss on her forehead. "Okay, little Izzy, you be a good girl, too, and do well in school. I've missed you and will visit you and your sister soon."

"I hope so, Daddy," Isabella said, hugging him hard one last time before saying more goodbyes to her brothers and sisters, then clasping Johanna's hand as they hoisted themselves up in the truck that would take them back to the little dim house on Seventh Street.

CHAPTER TWELVE

*"There is no friend than a sister, and there is no better
sister than you."*

The drive back home with Johanna was long, hot, and full of tension, it seemed, between Johanna and their mother. The fact that they had to all squeeze in the front seat didn't help matters. Howard seemed aware of the tense environment as well, and when they neared the road to their neighborhood, he said, "I'm going to fill this truck up at that gas station you like, Isabella. The one with the chocolate soda."

"Can we get some?" Isabella asked, clapping her hands as he said yes. She turned to Johanna. "This chocolate soda is the best! The times I had it I thought of you and how you'd love it, and now you're here."

Johanna laughed, hugging Isabella to her, and even their mother smiled.

The chocolate soda turned out to be just as delicious as Isabella remembered, and she laughed as Johanna gulped hers down, wiped her mouth with her free hand, then set the bottle on the stoop of the gas station.

"That was amazing," she said, letting out a loud burp accidentally.

Both girls busted out laughing, and when they'd all piled back into the truck, the ride home seemed much more pleasant.

"Well, do we have to still sleep on the couch?" Johanna whispered to Isabella as their mother and Howard were engaged in a discussion.

"I'm afraid so," Isabella answered.

"If you haven't noticed, I've grown up quite a bit since we've been apart. I think I'd rather sleep on the floor than try to squeeze on the couch."

"Don't be silly, Jo Jo," Isabella said. "We can still fit on the couch."

"Now who's being silly?" Johanna asked, winking as Isabella brushed off her comment.

"Let's just give it a try and see."

"Deal."

When they arrived at the house and went to sleep that night, Isabella had been right. Since she was still very petite, Johanna was able to curl up to her on the couch and both girls were able to sleep. Johanna had still grumbled that she hated being back to the dark box-like house, but being with Isabella eased her angst.

The following days turned to ordinary weeks for Isabella and Johanna. Johanna had finally started to become used to the dismal routine of the dreary little house and school. She enjoyed spending time with Sergei and Edwin and had just mentioned to Isabella that life was much better without Grandmother Swain when the unthinkable happened—Grandmother Swain returned.

"Sister, dear, bend near, so I can whisper my secret in your ear."

Isabella leaned in.

"I heard a rumor in school today by Junior that Grandmother Swain is coming back and she's bringing friends to stay on her property in a trailer!"

"Oh no!" Isabella cried, clutching her stomach. "I hope this isn't true, Johanna. And a trailer? Momma said only white trash live in trailers."

And true to Johanna's announcement, within a week, a van pulled into their neighborhood and parked in front of Grandmother Swain's old house.

"I wish Lottie wasn't leaving us soon," Juliana commented to Howard as she peeked beneath the front door blind. "I'm happy that she's at least letting Sergei and Edwin finish the school year. Oh my! Look at your cranky old mother. As spindly and mean-looking as ever! And who does she have with her? Were you serious when you said that the trailer on her lot is going to be used by two of her friends? And who are they? They look weird and creepy as hell!"

Isabella hadn't heard all of her stepdad's answers, but within a few days, everything happened just like Juliana had questioned him about. Grandmother Swain returned home. Aunt Lottie had left, and there were two strangers living on Grandmother Swain's property in a trailer.

And it didn't take long for Grandmother Swain to show her rotten old self again, Isabella thought as a few days later when she and Johanna were walking on their lawn to their porch, another confrontation happened.

She had been holding a Clark candy bar she'd won in a Spelling Bee when Grandmother Swain spotted them from her house and came outside.

"Hold it right there," she said, motioning for Isabella to stop walking. "Where did you get that Clark Bar? Are you the one stealing the candy bars from Junior's lunch?"

"Keep walking," Johanna told her, "we'll be inside soon."

"I said stop walking, you insolent brat!"

Johanna tugged Isabella along, but within seconds a blunt force knocked her down from behind. Grandmother Swain had hit her with her cane and was about to strike her again but Johanna blocked the cane with her arm. At that moment, Juliana pulled up to the curb in Howard's truck. She stormed out of the vehicle, shouting, "Don't you dare lay another hand on my daughter, you old witch!"

"She's a thief!" Grandmother Swain yelled back. "She's been stealing Junior's candy at school."

"If that's the case then I will punish her when I find it necessary," Juliana snapped. "Do I make myself clear?"

Grandmother Swain snorted, her close-knit murky eyes leveling on Isabella first then Johanna then back to Juliana. "These two will grow up to be nothing more than tramps. Mark my words."

"My children will never be like your granddaughters," Juliana told her. "Your granddaughters would drop their drawers for any man that would buy them a drink."

"You just wait until my son comes home," Grandmother Swain sneered. "He'll straighten you and those brats of yours out."

"Yeah. He'll straighten all of us out!" Juliana laughed. "He'll be so damn drunk all he'll do is go to sleep. If I didn't work, our whole house would starve and your pockets would be empty, too, since you're always asking for money."

"Why you little bitch," Grandmother Swain snapped back, stepping towards Juliana. "He could've done a lot better than you. I knew he was reaching in the bottom of the barrel, but he wouldn't listen to me since you had him between the legs."

Johanna squeezed Isabella's hand and whispered, "Look at Momma's face. She's going to let that old witch have it!"

Within minutes, their mother let out a long line of curse words and then the final blow.

"Bottom of the barrel, huh?" she told Grandmother Swain. "That's what you are. Don't think for one minute I don't know all about you having an affair behind your husband's back with Gino Nevel! Poor Howard looks nothing like your husband, but is the spitting image of poor ol' Gino. Maybe someone should wise Howard up to the truth!"

Grandmother Swain's face turned a beet red, and Isabella noticed another throbbing bluish vein she hadn't seen before in her grandmother's wrinkled neck. "You better shut that lying mouth if you know what's good for you!"

"I'll shut my mouth when you stop harassing my children!"

Swallowing hard, Grandmother Swain glanced at Isabella and Johanna and then turned abruptly away and stormed off as quickly as she could manage into her home.

"You girls go inside and wash up for dinner," Juliana said, following behind them as they walked into their home.

"Thank you for defending us, Momma," Isabella told her, rubbing her shoulder where she'd taken the hit, but her mother just shrugged and turned away.

"Silly Izzy," Johanna whispered to her. "She doesn't really care about us. How many times do I have to tell you that? It's all about pride with Momma. She doesn't want anyone taking away her authority to discipline us."

Isabella shook her head, hoping that what Johanna said wasn't true. She loved their mother, and sometimes she wondered why Johanna seemed determined to prove that their mother didn't really care about them.

Howard arrived through the porch door, his loud burp shaking Isabella from her depressing thoughts. *Momma had been right after all*, Isabella thought, noticing Howard's squinty eyes and the way he stumbled when he walked. He was drunk.

"Hey girls," he said, slumping onto the couch. "My mom's cousin Berna and her boyfriend are moving in next door in that trailer. I want you both to be respectful. Do you understand?"

Both Isabella and Johanna nodded. He quickly fell asleep, his snoring loud and obstructed as if he had a softball lodged in his throat.

"Great. Just great," Johanna mumbled. "Now where will we sleep if he doesn't wake up?"

"We'll figure something out," Isabella answered, tilting her head to look at Johanna.

That night when Howard didn't wake up, Isabella and Johanna slept on the kitchen floor with their blankets and arms wrapped around each other for warmth. School dawned too early for both of them, and by the time they returned home, Johanna was pressing into Isabella and telling her to bend her ear.

"Grandmother Swain's cousin is now in the trailer. She's an old maid and used to be a school teacher but is retired now," Johanna told Isabella. "Grandmother Swain, that old hag, is her last living relative." Johanna giggled, then whispered a few more juicy tidbits of information. "I heard Momma telling Howard that Berna is an alcoholic and the school kicked her out because of it. Momma also said that Berna's boyfriend, Gale, is an ugly thing too and creepy. I spotted him the other day looking in our kitchen window, but didn't know who he was. Have you seen him yet, Izzy?"

Izzy put her hand over her mouth. She did remember an ugly old man looking at her the other day from behind the bushes. Slowly bringing her hand away from her mouth, she said, "I did, Johanna! He's horrible. He was hiding behind the bushes."

"I hate living here, Izzy," Johanna said. "It gets creepier all the time."

They both walked into the kitchen, finding the cabinets bare again of any real food.

"I sure do miss living with Daddy," Johanna said.

"I do too," Isabella agreed, and they both hugged each other close.

A week later, on a sunny Saturday morning, Isabella burst through the front door of their home, searching frantically for Johanna. She found her sister sitting at the kitchen table putting a puzzle together. Out of breath, she slumped into the other chair.

Johanna hurried to her. "What is it?" she asked, smoothing Isabella's bangs from her forehead. "What happened?"

"Wait. I need to catch my breath," Isabella told her.

Johanna walked to the sink and poured Johanna a glass of water. Bringing it to her, she said, "Here, Izzy, sip. Aunda said sipping water can calm us."

Isabella took the glass of water, sipped a few times, breathed deeply, then closed her eyes. "Shut and lock the front door, Johanna, before Momma or Howard return."

Johanna did exactly as her sister asked and then returned to her side. "Now you must tell me, Izzy!"

Isabella nodded. "Sister, dear, bend near, so I can whisper my secret in your ear."

Johanna knelt on the floor beside Isabella and put her head to Isabella's chest.

"Never tell this secret to anyone, Jo Jo. Grandmother Swain will call me a liar."

"Don't be silly! I never tell our secrets to anyone," Johanna reminded. "You are the dearest person in my whole life."

"I know," Isabella said, closing her eyes a second and then opening them to look at Isabella. "I'm just reminding you to be careful. I don't want to get into trouble."

"Well, you're gonna get into trouble with me unless you tell me!"

Isabella took a deep breath, exhaled, and then shared her secret. "When I was coming home from the library today, Grandmother Swain was shouting at me to take some homemade soup to Berna because Berna wasn't feeling well. Even though I knew that ugly old Berna and her boyfriend probably had a hangover, I knew I had to do it or Howard would be mad. I took the soup over to Berna's and she asked me to butter some bread for her and give her a glass of water."

"So where's the secret?" Johanna shrugged. "That's no secret!"

"I'm not finished," Isabella defended, wringing her hands.

"Well, now, I know you aren't finished and something really bad happened," Johanna told her, "because you only wring your hands like that when something horrible happened."

Isabella nodded and breathed deeply then exhaled. "So I gave her the bread and water, and then Gale asked me from the other room if I saw the new Look magazine with the picture of Betty Grable on the front cover. I hadn't seen it so I told him no. He told me to come in the other room where he was and sit by him so he could show me and we could read the article together." Isabella could feel the tears start to form in her eyes. "I sat down beside him and he put his arm around my shoulder, telling me to hold part of the magazine while he held the other so I did. I started turning the pages when Gale let go of his side and put his hand on my pee-pee. I jumped up and ran out of the room and told Berna that I had to go home for dinner. I ran so fast to get out of the trailer and back here."

Johanna's face changed to one that frightened Isabella. She hoped her sister wasn't mad at her. "I knew it!" Johanna shouted. "He's a pervert!"

Isabella tilted her head, glad that her sister was mad at Gale and not her. "What's a pervert?"

"It's when a grown man touches little girls! He's a child molester! That's what he is!"

"How do you know what all these words mean, Johanna?"

"Because you might read a lot of school books to get good grades, but I have street smarts, Izzy. I pay attention and that helps me stay out of trouble and it helps protect you. Now, listen carefully to me," Johanna said, pulling Isabella's hand inside her own. "The next time Grandmother Swain asks you to take something over to Berna's trailer, you must find me first and I'll go over with you. I will make damn sure you will never be around him by yourself."

"Okay, I will find you, but stop cussing."

"That word is only one of many I could use on a pervert like Gale. I've learned a lot of new curse words from that boy I like at school. Do you know who he is?"

"I remember him. He's that Italian boy. He seems really nice, but wouldn't Momma be mad if she found out you two were liking each other?"

Johanna huffed and rolled her eyes. "Well, she's never gonna know now, is she?"

Isabella shook her head. "I'm not going to tell, but I sure hope you don't get in trouble, Jo Jo."

"No worries, Izzy."

"Sometimes you just seem so much older than I am," Isabella said, wishing she were more like her sister. "Even though you're only two years older, it's as if you were already in high school."

Johanna grinned, letting go of Isabella's hand to pat her on the top of the head. "Listen, Izzy, you should never want to be someone else. Not even me. Every year we get older, and soon we'll be able to get out of this hell hole here."

Isabella sighed. How she would love to never be around Grandmother Swain and all of the terrible people like Berna and Gale. "Sometimes I think I'm the meanest person in the world because I hate Grandmother Swain so much, Johanna." Thinking back on to the horrible things Grandmother Swain had done to her, she grew angry. "Remember how she made you drink Epsom Salt water because she told you it would clear your complexion? She forced you to drink that awful stuff all the time, as if she really cared about your complexion!"

Johanna nodded, her face reddening. "I remember. I'd like to force that drink down the old witch's throat now and see how she likes it."

Isabella decided to confess a secret to Johanna. "You know what, Johanna? I hate her. I wish she was dead so many times. Is that terrible? Am I going to hell?"

Johanna hugged Isabella. "Of course not! But don't let it fester in you, Izzy. You go to church and love God, and He knows the terrible things that are happening. Let God deal with Grandmother Swain and Junior and all of them. But you're only human. You're gonna feel angry."

Isabella let out a huge sigh of relief. "Oh, Johanna, thank you! I feel so much better."

"That's what sisters are for."

Isabella smiled. "We are the BEST of sisters, the BEST of friends."

"You got that right," Johanna laughed, "and we'll be together always."

"Always," Isabella repeated and then they made plans for the rest of their day, each focusing on the moment when the future still seemed so uncertain.

CHAPTER THIRTEEN

"There is no friend than a sister, and there is no better sister than you."

"We might be moving again," Juliana told Isabella and Johanna two weeks later. "I'm not certain, but it's a possibility."

Howard walked into the kitchen where all three women were and overheard the conversation. "Maybe it wouldn't be a possibility if you didn't throw a plate of mashed potatoes at my father on the day he returned home." Howard shook his head. "It was supposed to be a celebration. Hell, you girls didn't even know my mother was still married!"

"Maybe your father should've kept his mouth shut about disciplining my girls. He listened to your old hag of a mother about them and tried to tell me how to raise them." Juliana turned away from Howard and laughed. "He sure did look funny with mashed potatoes and gravy all over his face and blood dripping down his nose from where the plate smacked him."

"It's no wonder I drink as much as I do, having to deal with your outbursts," Howard said and then put up his hand when Juliana was going to argue. "Please, don't. No arguments. I'm tired."

He turned his back on the women in the kitchen and walked outside to the front porch, most likely to smoke a cigarette.

Johanna grabbed Isabella's hand and squeezed, leaning in to whisper. "That was the funniest thing I've ever seen when Momma flung that plate of mashed potatoes. The only thing that could've made it better would've been if Howard's stupid dad would've ducked and it struck Grandmother Swain in the head!"

Isabella burst out laughing, covering her mouth when her mother turned to her.

"What's so funny?"

"Nothing, Momma," Isabella said, wondering why her mother went into so many mood swings.

Juliana studied both of her daughters before looking at Johanna. "Tonight I want to talk to you, young lady. You understand?"

Johanna nodded and Isabella grew scared. When their mother had left the room to find Howard, Isabella turned to her. "What is it? Why does she want to speak with you?"

"I don't know," Johanna said, her brows drawn together as if in deep thought. "Maybe she knows about me and Dominic."

"Oh, Johanna! That would be horrible!"

"Stop worrying!" Johanna snapped, and by her agitation, Isabella knew she was worried too.

"I'll try."

They both left the house to find their cousins to play a game of hide and seek, but the whole time, Isabella couldn't shake a terrible feeling that Johanna was in deep trouble.

The hours passed too quickly, and before long, it was evening. Dinner was one potato and an ear of corn which had been roasted outside on the fire pit that Howard had lit earlier. He opened a bottle of cheap liquor and disappeared outside somewhere. Meanwhile, Juliana told Johanna she wanted to talk with her.

Isabella hid by the archway to the kitchen, listening.

"I'll make this quick," Juliana said. "You love to read like Isabella, don't you?"

"Yes," Johanna answered.

"What are your absolute favorite books? Name two of them."

"*Tom Sawyer* and *A Christmas Carol* by Dickens."

"You have those here?"

"Yes," Johanna replied.

"Bring them to me."

Johanna left the kitchen and her quick gaze to Isabella said she didn't know what was going on. She clearly looked confused. A few minutes later, she had the two books with her and entered the kitchen again.

"Isabella, you might as well come in here too instead of eavesdropping," Juliana said.

Isabella's face grew red from embarrassment as she entered the kitchen and stood beside Johanna.

"Now give me the books," Juliana commanded to Johanna, and Johanna handed them to her. "Well, now," she said, "I hear that you and a boy named Dominic have been seeing each other behind my back. You realize that he's a wop and not someone I would want you to be associated with?"

Johanna's posture tensed, and Isabella could feel the anger and fear radiating from her.

"He's a nice boy," she told their mother. "He holds my books while we walk to classes and he's always been respectful. His family is kind like he is."

Their mother laughed, and Isabella realized in that moment how a little laugh could be one of the ugliest sounds. "He's a wop. And so is his family. You are not to see him anymore, and be thankful that I am not going to punish you. However, follow me."

Both Johanna and Isabella followed her outside to where she stood by the fire pit. The moon and stars shone brightly, beautifully, but it was not a balmy night to be enjoyed.

116

"Watch what happens when you disobey me," Juliana said, moving her hands to toss the books in the fire with both her daughters screaming "NO," but it was too late. The books landed on top of the hot coals, and then Juliana quickly grabbed a nearby can of gasoline, dousing the books, and swoosh, the flames rose up, engulfing the books to nothing more than ashes.

Isabella burst out crying, but Johanna stood still as if in a trance. She kept her gaze on her beloved burning books, and then when they were no more than ashes, she turned to Juliana, stared at her and then turned and walked away.

Their mother seemed surprised that Johanna hadn't said anything. She gave a nervous little giggle then looked at Isabella. "Well, then. Learn from this, Isabella, because if you ever disobey me, something you love, too, will disappear."

Isabella nodded and walked back into the house, wanting to console her sister. When she located her sitting at the kitchen table and putting together pieces of a puzzle, she grew confused. "Aren't you sad, Johanna?"

Johanna shrugged. "I'm sad that we don't have a mother that loves us, Izzy. I'm sad that many kids have better homes than we do, but you know what I'm not sad about? I'm not sad that I have you at least. We have each other, and one day we'll be grown and won't have to live here any longer."

"But I think Momma does love us," Isabella pointed out. But even as she said the words, she wondered why they seemed so hollow, as if they were nothing but air and carried no weight.

"You are a dreamer," Johanna said, snapping a puzzle piece in place. "Why not dream of what we will become in life? Let us be educated, rich, happy and in love. I want us to be successful, Izzy, and when I've found a way out, I'm taking it and then I'll come back for you. We must remember never to let mean people break our spirit— the thing that makes us us."

Johanna's words sounded beautiful. As beautiful as a time long ago on Miss Aunda's farm.

"You know what else?" Johanna asked, not waiting for an answer, and then she looked around and whispered, "Sister, dear, bend near, so I can whisper my secret in your ear."

Isabella smiled and leaned in.

"I don't think Edwin is our cousin, but our brother! I always see the loving way Juliana talks to him, and I heard her telling Lottie that she was happy to have a son."

"No! That can't be!" Isabella said. "Why wouldn't she tell us or raise him herself?"

"Who knows? But that may be happening soon because when Lottie leaves, Edwin is coming to live with us permanently but Sergei is going with Aunt Lottie."

"I like Edwin, though, and I feel bad that he only has Junior to play with."

"I like Edwin too, but I feel bad only for us. We are second-best to him."

"This is a lot to think about," Isabella said. "I think I'm going to bed."

"Good night, sweet Izzy," Johanna said. "Say your prayers."

"I will. I'll pray that someone gives you two new books that Momma burned tonight, and I pray that we get older and leave this place real soon."

"Sounds like a great prayer, sister," Johanna said. "Now go to sleep."

And Isabella did just as she was told, but her heart was heavy.

―✸―

"Izzy, wake up!" Johanna told her. "It's Sunday and you wanted to go to church, remember? Plus, Edwin and Sergei want you to catch their baseballs after church in the field next door."

Isabella awoke slowly. "Yes, you're right. I want to go to church. Will you go with me?"

"No. I don't think church does much good for someone like me anymore."

"Oh, but Johanna, you must! Gale was following me in his car the last time I walked home. Sergei and Edwin showed up right when Gale was going to get out of the car. You know he drives like a maniac and he asked if he could take us all home. I thought that was okay since Sergei and Edwin were with me, but he kept slamming on the brakes and we hit the dashboard a few times. When we finally got out, Edwin and Sergei asked if they'd see him later, and he said no, but then whispered to me that he'd be seeing me only!"

Johanna got angry. "What a perverted ass! Well, I'll go with you one Sunday a month, Izzy, and then we'll figure out something for the other three, okay? Maybe even Sergei and Edwin can help."

"Thank you!"

"No need to thank me, Izzy! We're sisters and I love you. Now, you probably should get ready or you'll be late."

Isabella did just that, and both of them enjoyed a wonderful church service. Later that day, Sergei and Edwin were playing baseball and asked Isabella to retrieve the baseballs that landed in the outfield.

"I don't want to just do that," she told them. "Teach me to play and to hit the ball."

Both boys laughed. "Girls don't play Little League! They don't play any sports. Just go get the balls we hit!"

"I'm not doing anything until you both teach me how to play!" Isabella shouted, placing her hands on her hips.

"Boy, when did you get so sassy? You were always so shy."

"Okay, okay," said Sergei. "We'll teach you, but let's hurry because it's Edwin and I that have to practice for the Little League Championship."

That afternoon, they taught Isabella how to hit, both being surprised by her ability to strike the ball clear into the outfield and beyond.

"Man! You're really good!" Edwin said. "Especially for a girl!"

"Maybe girls are better than boys at baseball," she told them, and they both started laughing and hitting each other playfully from that comment. "Yeah, right! Like girls can do anything better than boys!"

Isabella rolled her eyes, happy that she'd showed both of them that she not only could hit the baseball, but she could run the bases quickly as well. It was times like these, when the sun was shining, and she'd been to church, that her world seemed brighter and not as filled with so many dark, evil people.

And then Junior showed up, holding a pen knife and asking them if he could play too.

"No way," Sergei said. "We're teaching Isabella and then we have to practice."

Junior ignored them, walking past them to pick up the bat on the ground. He lifted it and swung it around, almost hitting Isabella in the head. When Sergei and Edwin yelled at him, he flipped his pen knife open, started walking away, and then moved his hand quickly down, striking Sergei in the leg.

Blood spurted and Isabella started screaming right along with Sergei and Edwin. Juliana, Howard, and Grandmother Swain all ran outside their houses and to the children.

"I fell!" Junior said, starting to cry. "They wouldn't let me play with them and I started walking away but they pushed me and I fell into Sergei with my knife!"

"Why you rotten kids!" Grandmother Swain said, turning towards Sergei, Isabella, and Edwin. "That's what you get for being mean!"

"Are you insane?" Juliana told her. "Look at this wound! We've got to get Sergei to the hospital. It's going to take at least six stitches! Your Junior is a monster, you old hag!"

Junior started crying louder, and Sergei started moaning with pain. Howard scooped him up in his arms, placed him in the truck with Edwin and Juliana, and headed to the hospital. Isabella watched the truck disappear around the corner and then turned to walk away when she heard Junior laughing with Grandmother Swain.

"I wish they were dead," she whispered aloud, saying a prayer for Sergei and wondering if bad wishes on people made prayers go unanswered.

Three hours later, Juliana, Howard, and Sergei returned from the hospital. It had taken eight stitches to close his wound.

Isabella and he walked outside to the woods where Edwin met them. Sergei limped a bit and told them he had every intention of still playing in the Little League Championship game.

"I hate him," he told Edwin and her. "Junior is going to end up in prison one day. He's crazy, and everyone is school and here knows it."

"I wish he was in prison already," Isabella said, shaking her head. "But not only him, but Grandmother Swain and Gale."

"They are horrible people. I hate them all."

Isabella felt better just hearing both boys say the same things she was feeling. Maybe she wasn't so bad after all in how she thought of them.

They talked some more, each finding comfort in the other's recollections of horrible events. Laughter rang out with the story about Juliana throwing the plate of mashed potatoes, and Isabella decided that on that happy note, she'd leave and head for home. Certainly, Johanna would be waiting to hear all about the events of the day.

Sure enough, Johanna was waiting for her as she entered the house. "Izzy! What happened?"

Isabella shook her head and rolled her eyes. "It was crazy!" And then she proceeded to tell her sister all the facts of the afternoon. Once she finished, Johanna grew quiet.

"Poor Sergei. I bet that's gonna screw him up from running the bases."

"Maybe, but he's determined to do his best."

"That's good," Johanna smiled. "I'll pray for him."

"I love hearing you say that," Isabella told her. "I hardly hear you talk of God anymore, and you know how much I love him and how much he loves us."

"Well, did you ever wonder why if he loved us so much, why he'd let us have to live this way?"

"What do you mean?" Isabella asked, thinking she knew already but wanted Johanna to explain it.

"Okay, Izzy," Johanna said, reaching down and pulling one of her shoes off. "Go on, pull one of your shoes off, too."

Isabella did that.

"Now, turn it over and look at the bottom. Really look at it," Johanna said. "Look at all the holes and where you and I cut and pasted pieces of cardboard to them. Do you think Juliana cares for us now? She doesn't care whether we have decent clothes or shoes. But what she does care about, is that she secretly gave money to Howard to buy Edwin new shoes. She only cares about him for whatever reason. And it's not only her, Isabella. Daddy cares only for Stella. He makes certain she has beautiful clothes and strong shoes, too. Did you know that he bought a house for Estelle and her new husband? He actually did! And all they do is rent it off of him. And do you know why he did that? So that when Stella goes to school, she can stay in the same neighborhood as him. Isn't that something? He cares so much for her but nothing for us anymore. We don't have anyone but each other. And did you ever notice that we don't get invited to any classmate's sleepovers? Do you know why? Because we go to school with a bunch of rich kids and we are dirt poor. It's always been me and you against the world, and I'm making this promise to you, Isabella. One day, we'll show those rich school bitches up because not only do we have love for one another, but we'll each be successful one day. Just wait and see. We'll show all of them."

A deep confusion filled Isabella. She loved Johanna's positivity that they'd be successful and rich, but she didn't know what to think about why they were poor or why God allowed it. Or why their father didn't care for them any longer and why their mother secretly cared for Edwin. Somewhere in Johanna's heart, she'd changed her views on God.

She grew silent. Deep in thought.

"I'm sorry," Johanna told her, slipping her shoe back on and then lifting Isabella's chin with her fingers to look at her. "I know there is a God, Izzy. And I do believe he is a loving God. I'm not sure, either, why all of this happens, but for today, maybe we can just let it go, except that I'm going to call Daddy tomorrow and ask if he could buy us some clothes. I only have one bra, and it's torn and way too small. I'm bigger this year and the bra was from two years ago! I'll ask for you too, Izzy. But right now, let's focus on the good that I said. We will be rich one day. And we will always have each other. Always."

Isabella nodded and finally smiled. "Okay, Johanna. There are a lot of positive things to think on. You're right."

"And Isabella, we have nothing to lose any longer so I'm going to ask Daddy sometime too about college. I want to be a librarian because I love books so much. I'm going to ask him to pay for me to go to college and you should too. We need to make certain we have an education, Izzy. We've got to do that. Promise me you'll do that, okay?"

Isabella knew that there would be long years yet before they even graduated high school, but she promised anyway. After all, Johanna always did seem to know more about life, people and the future than she did.

"I promise."

"Good. Now let's find something to eat."

Isabella agreed, but knew that the cabinets would most likely be bare once again.

CHAPTER FOURTEEN

"Side by side or miles apart we are sisters connected by the heart."

The next day dawned early for both girls as they were told to perform house chores. After sweeping the kitchen floor, Johanna peeked outside the front window to see their mother and Howard leaving in the truck.

"Quick! Hurry here, Isabella," she summoned, walking to the phone inside their mother's room. "Let's call Daddy about school clothes."

Isabella hurried to her side, watching as her sister dialed the number to Estelle's house. "Hello? Estelle? This is Johanna. Do you have my dad's new phone number?"

Isabella couldn't hear Estelle, but Johanna mumbled the words: "She's drunk."

Isabella covered her mouth as she started to laugh. She knew it wasn't funny that Estelle had a drinking problem, but the fact that she was drunk and talking to her sister was comical.

"Why do I want to know?" Johanna said into the phone. "You mean you'll only tell me if I tell you why?"

A few more minutes ticked by with Johanna telling Estelle that they needed new clothes. She then held the phone out to Isabella to hear as Estelle started shouting that their father had been paying their mother child support.

"Tell that hag of a mother of yours to stop spending the money on herself and buy you kids some decent clothes!" Estelle then gave Johanna their dad's new number, wished them well, and hung up.

"So Mom is getting money," Johanna said, looking disgusted. "I really am starting to hate her, Izzy."

"Johanna, don't say that. Please. We've got to keep our hearts like God wants us to. You read so many books, don't you see those dreams in those books? They are full of hope, and one day we will have beautiful clothes and live in a beautiful home just like you told me days ago. We'll be successful and happy. God will care for us, but we have to have faith and pray to God and ask him to bless me and you. Don't forget that God does answer prayers."

Johanna just looked at her, rolled her eyes, and dialed their father's number. "Well, let's see if God answers this one." His landlady answered, and Johanna left a message asking if she can have their father call them. "Okay," she told Isabella after she replaced the receiver. "Now let's see if Daddy calls us back." She then tousled Isabella's hair and said, "I have something to tell you."

"You do?"

Johanna grinned, her beautiful green eyes lighting up. "Sister, dear, bend near, so I can whisper my secret in your ear."

Isabella giggled, clapping her hands and leaning in.

"Dominic and I are still seeing each other. And I want to see him next Saturday. Can you ask Juliana today if we can go swimming next Saturday when it's free for school kids? She likes you better than me."

Isabella saw the tears suddenly well in Johanna's eyes for the first time in a long time when talking about their mother. Her heart broke. "She loves you, too, Johanna. It's just that you seem to do things a lot that she doesn't like."

"Yeah, like breathe," Johanna said, shrugging. "Isabella, I can't live with no happiness. She makes me feel like that caged rabbit Gale caught the other day. I don't think God meant for parents to be so hard on their children. I want to be happy and smile. Not live afraid and alone like she, Junior, and Grandmother Swain want us to."

"I think I'm starting to understand you better, Johanna," Isabella told her, feeling as though she truly was starting to understand how damaging suppressing someone so lively and beautiful like Johanna could be. Johanna referred to it as a caged rabbit, but Isabella remembered the beautiful Monarch butterfly Junior had caught one day and then pinned its wings to a tree.

That's more of how she thought of Johanna. A free spirit. Beautiful. Meant to fly and live. Not be trapped or pinned.

"I'll help you," she told her sister, laughing when Johanna hugged her tight. "I'll ask Momma today if we can go swimming next Saturday."

"Oh, thank you! Thank you!" Johanna exclaimed, twirling around the room as if ballroom dancing.

She grabbed Isabella's hands in one movement and then they both danced together, pretending to be a grand couple in a grand mansion surrounded by people who loved them.

Juliana lowered the newspaper slowly that evening when Isabella approached her.

"So what time of day are you girls thinking of going?" she asked Isabella, glancing at Johanna who stood nearby.

"Probably ten a.m.," Isabella answered. "Can we go?"

Juliana studied first Isabella's face then Johanna's. "Okay, you both can go but only until six. Then you need to be home. And one more thing. Don't let me catch either of you around that wop Dominic. Do you understand?"

Isabella started trembling until Johanna hurried over to her and ushered her back into the kitchen. "Stop it," she whispered. "Stop acting so nervous."

"I didn't hear an answer, girls," their mother said, picking up the newspaper to read it again.

"Yes," they both said. "We understand."

"Good," she replied, and then dismissed them as if they didn't exist.

Johanna tugged at Isabella. "Let's go outside. Quick."

They both rushed outdoors and down their walkway into the woods nearby. "Phew," Johanna said, smiling. "That was a close one! But we did it! *You* did it! We can go! Oh, thank you, Izzy!"

"Thank me?" Isabella said, shaking her head. "Momma's gonna kill us if we talk to that wop."

"Don't call him that!"

Isabella raised her eyebrows. "I don't even know what a wop is!"

"It means With Out Papers," Johanna told her. "Like when people come from another country to the United States, but don't do it legally."

"Ahhh, I see," Isabella said. "Is he one?"

"No," Johanna defended, and then her green eyes became soft as if she were thinking happy thoughts. "His family is a hard-working family and kind. Very nice people. They do have papers, but many people want to believe all Italians are here illegally."

"I feel bad for them then," Isabella said, pondering all that Johanna was explaining to her.

"I do too," Johanna agreed. "Dominic's family is just like he is. They are so great, Isabella. They offer me food as soon as I walk into the door, and they ask me how I am doing and they treat me like I matter. I love Italians because of them. They are truly great, kind people, and I think I love Dominic."

"Oh please! Don't say that!" Isabella cried. "If Momma finds out, we'll both be whipped raw!"

"Well, she's not going to then, but I am so happy about next Saturday!"

That week went by fast for Isabella, but her sister couldn't count the days fast enough. When Saturday finally arrived, they both were given a few pennies to take the bus to the pool so that Juliana didn't have to stop reading her *True Romance* magazine in order to drive them.

When they got to the park, Johanna started to look frantically around for Dominic, and they spotted him at the front entrance.

"He's here!" exclaimed Johanna, running towards him.

"Don't go so fast," Isabella said, but Johanna was already motioning for Dominic to follow them to a private spot at the park where picnic benches were set up. Dominic walked over and hugged Johanna.

"Dominic! Please don't hug my sister in public! We have a lot of cousins that come to this pool. We don't want to get into trouble," Isabella told him, wringing her hands.

"Trouble for what?" he asked, shaking his head and looking confused. "What is so bad about two people liking one another? Love is a great thing, little Izzy."

"Oh, not you too!" Isabella snapped, rolling her eyes. "So love is going to protect us from a whipping? I doubt it. And please don't call me Izzy. I don't like that name from anyone but my sister."

He grinned, and it was such a charming smile that Isabella immediately knew why her sister had fallen in love with him. He was kind, handsome, and smart. She could see all those qualities in him already, so what was so bad about Italians that people like their mother wanted nothing to do with them?

"Okay, Isabella. I'm sorry. I won't call you Izzy anymore," Dominic apologized. "I only meant it in a good way."

All of a sudden, Isabella didn't mind if he did call her that.

"Don't you start liking him too," Johanna laughed, tapping her arm a little.

Isabella's cheeks flushed with embarrassment.

"Come with us on a walk," Johanna told her. "We're going to go on that path that follows the creek nearby."

Isabella declined the offer. Not only was she embarrassed at what Johanna had said, but she didn't want to follow two lovebirds walking hand-in-hand and possibly getting them all in a lot of trouble.

She watched them walk towards the path as she herself started down a hill towards the pool. It was then when she saw their mother's new used Buick pull up to the curb. "Oh, my God! Please God, *no!*" Isabella said aloud, turning around and running as quickly as she could towards where Johanna and Dominic disappeared to.

Spotting them ahead, she hollered and they both came running back. Out of breath, Isabella pointed behind her. "Momma is here. Get him out of here. Run, Dominic!"

Dominic looked at Johanna as if he needed her approval.

She looked past Isabella's head to the pool below then turned back to him. "Run!"

And off he went into the woods, turning around once to mouth the words, *I love you*, to Johanna.

"Quick, Isabella," Johanna said, pointing to the picnic bench. "Let's go over there. And here, open this poetry book and act like you're reading it to me. Juliana will find us soon enough, but she'll be mad that she had to walk all this way up this hill. Just watch."

They both hustled to the clearing where the picnic bench was and sat down on it with Johanna sitting on the grass by Isabella's feet.

Isabella opened the book and began to read.

About ten minutes later, their mother spotted them and started walking up the hill towards them. "There you girls are! I've been looking everywhere for you and I'm not happy I had to walk up that damn hill."

Johanna winked at Isabella.

"Hi Momma," Isabella greeted, trying to hide her nervous hands since she couldn't wring them together or her mother would know something was wrong.

Juliana looked at both of them. "Okay, so where is that wop? I got a telephone call saying you both were seen with him, and that you, Johanna, were walking with him."

Isabella kept quiet, knowing that her stomach would not allow her to talk or she'd vomit.

Johanna, however, looked as casual as anything as if there was not a care in the world.

"There was no boy walking with us. Whoever called you must've been mistaken. The only one here with us was Francis Vernon earlier. You remember her, don't you? She's the girl who just got a short DA haircut that everyone is laughing about because she looks like a boy!"

"Where is she now?" their mother asked, looking as if she was believing Johanna.

"Her dad picked her up at the bottom of the hill about a half hour ago. You can ask him if she was here. He'll tell you she was."

Their mother nodded, obviously sold on the story that Johanna presented. Isabella let out a silent sigh of relief. Somehow, her sister had perfected the skill of lying.

"Well, get your asses in the car anyway," their mother said. "I didn't come all this way to turn around and head back empty-handed."

"But we didn't even get to swim yet!" Isabella told her, but then quickly stood and followed her with Johanna down the hill to the car.

Johanna looked as happy as a lark, sitting in the back seat and looking past the window to the woods near the horizon.

No doubt she was thinking of Dominic, Isabella thought, and although it was terrible to go through so much trouble and anguish, she was still happy for her sister.

Squeezing her hand then leaning down on Johanna's shoulder, she asked, "What's a DA haircut?"

Johanna busted out laughing. "It means Duck's Ass."

Isabella laughed too, thankful that they weren't in trouble, and thankful once again that they had each other.

Later that evening, Juliana said, "Hey girls. Do you know who it was who told me that you were walking with that wop? It was Priscilla. She's back for the weekend and called me."

Both Isabella and Johanna remained quiet.

"And now she's going to pay the price for trying to stir up trouble."

Johanna tugged Isabella's hand to follow her outside. Once there, she said, "Juliana is going to give it to Priscilla just like she did to Ann Bailey, that old witch. Remember that, Izzy?"

"No, I don't remember. What happened?"

"I can't believe you don't remember! Ann Bailey put you with your fair skin into the sun during a heat wave! She watched you fry and blocked me from helping you! You ended up in the hospital. Then someone showed up at our house when Daddy was working one day and beat the hell out of Ann. She ended up almost dying. It was Juliana who beat her."

"Ugh! I do kind of remember that, but maybe it's best if I don't."

Johanna nodded. "Maybe." And then she shrugged and laughed. "Well, I think Priscilla is going to get a beating, too. Just wait and see."

At that moment, voices were heard coming from Junior's house. "Hurry, let's see what happening!" Johanna said, pulling Isabella alongside as they hid by the front porch of Junior's house. Their mother was inside shouting at Priscilla.

"It was them!" Priscilla shouted back. "Your daughters are tramps! And who can mistake them when Isabella has that snow-white hair and Johanna has that red mop! They are lying! Now, get out of our house, you bitch!"

"I'll get out of here," Juliana yelled. "And you can stay in this house with your insane son and hag of a mother!"

Howard appeared unnoticed and snuck up on Isabella and Johanna, telling them to go back home. They did exactly that, and as soon as they entered their house, their mother and Howard returned, too.

"So what the hell was that all about, Juliana? Do you want to end up in jail for assaulting my sister?"

"That no good sister and mother of yours are always trying to make my daughters look like sluts. My God, they are only nine and twelve years old!"

"Isabella," Johanna whispered to her as they sat on the couch listening to their mother and Howard. "Did you hear what she said about our ages? She doesn't even know how old we are! That's how much attention she pays to us. Neither you nor I ever had a birthday cake or party. That's another reason I won't call her "Momma" anymore. She's no mother."

Isabella lowered her eyes and stared at her hands neatly folded in her lap. Her mother and Howard's voices were still raised. Johanna reached over and grasped her hand.

"Don't worry, Izzy," she told her. "We always have each other. And when we get out of this place, we can have as many birthday parties as we want for one another."

Isabella smiled a little. The future would always be brighter with her sister by her side.

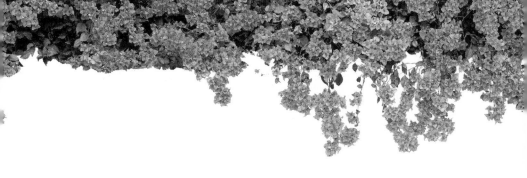

CHAPTER FIFTEEN

"A sister shares childhood memories and grown-up dreams."

The school year turned quickly into autumn. Isabella stared out of the front porch window, watching as Johanna neared and then entered the house. Johanna had been meeting Dominic behind one of the neighbor's houses, and Isabella had been wringing her hands in fear that they'd be caught.

Johanna was all smiles as she hugged Isabella. "You don't have to worry now. Everything is okay." And then she quickly glanced around the house before whispering, "Sister, dear, bend near, so I can whisper my secret in your ear."

Isabella leaned in once again.

"There are two things. Two really big things," Johanna said. "The first is that I'm going to sing a solo in the school's spring concert in April. The choir director said I have perfect pitch!" She twirled around a bit, then returned to Isabella's side, bending again near her ear. "The second secret is nasty but I've got to tell you. Juliana is having an affair!"

"What!"

"Shhh!" Johanna said. "Lower your voice."

Isabella found it difficult to do so. "Okay, Jo Jo, now tell me what you mean by that secret."

Johanna laughed a little and rolled her eyes. "It means she's cheating on Howard, and it's with Reynard—Howard's best friend!"

Isabella clapped her hand over her mouth. When she finally felt like she could control her surprise, she asked, "Are you sure? What makes you think that?"

"Isabella, have you ever noticed when Howard leaves for work, no matter what shift he's working, Reynard's green Ford pulls up to the driveway? Plus, the only time Juliana gives us money to go to the store for bread and milk is right before he shows up."

"Are you sure they're not just friends?"

"Isabella, you try to see the good in people all the time, but let me tell you, there are many rotten people that have no good in them. Do you think Grandmother Swain, Priscilla, Junior, or even Gale are good people? Not everyone is as nice as we are."

"Well," Isabella said, considering her sister's words. "Maybe you're right, but it's so creepy to think of Momma cheating on Howard."

"Then don't think about it anymore. Just be aware of it so you don't come home early someday and find them kissing—or worse!"

Isabella frowned, and Johanna tugged her chin upward. "Izzy, I know I joke around a lot, but I am serious. I think Juliana is. I also want to tell you that we should both focus on getting out of this house and miserable town as soon as high school is over."

"You've said that before," Isabella told her, remembering all the late-night talks they'd had through the years. "But it seems impossible sometimes."

Johanna nodded. "I feel that way too, but no matter what, we must both go to college. I'll probably go first since I'm older than you."

"You're only two and half years older, Johanna," Isabella said, not liking thoughts of Johanna leaving her.

"Listen, Izzy, you *must* go to college! Promise me, and I will, too. Now, when you go, what do you think you'd like to study? Or be when you grow up?"

134

Isabella thought about that a while. "I think I'd like to become a teacher or nurse."

"I knew you'd say that," Johanna said, shaking her head. "Because that's all women are who are educated, but there's more than that, you know. Think outside the box."

"Well, what about you?" Isabella asked her. "What are you thinking you'd like to become?"

"Anything I love to do or something that makes a lot of money. And I want to travel the world, with the first country I visit being Ireland. I've read so much about it in some of my favorite stories."

"You love books, Johanna," Isabella pointed out. "You mentioned becoming a librarian. Would you still like that?"

Johanna's green eyes flashed, and Isabella smiled. She'd hit on something her sister was passionate about. Books. "Oh, Johanna, you must become a librarian," she insisted.

"But I learned that librarians don't make much money...."

"Yeah, but they must make enough to support a good living, right? I mean, wouldn't that just be perfect for you?" Isabella asked.

"It would be, Izzy," Johanna smiled.

Isabella smiled back. She'd never seen such a full, beautiful smile on her sister before. She said a little prayer that God would help Johanna become a librarian.

"And maybe you can stay out of trouble till you graduate," Isabella added, giggling. "That whole day with Dominic almost made me sick!"

"Trouble?" Johanna laughed, playfully pushing Isabella's shoulder. "I don't get into trouble."

Isabella found that comment so hilarious, she started laughing. "Yes, you do! What about the strawberry caper you talked poor Sergei into? You ate all of Momma's strawberries at the movies instead of bringing them to her from the store. She was so mad!"

"She sure was," Johanna agreed, tilting her head and mentioning a few other times she'd gotten into trouble.

Both sisters talked for a while, laughing and recalling such memorable times, and then Isabella asked, "Johanna, do you really think Momma is going to leave Howard and run away with Reynard?"

"That's exactly what I think she'll do. Mark my words."

"Then what will happen to us if she does?" Those words weren't even out of Isabella's mouth yet before her stomach started aching. Gone was the laughter she had just shared with her sister. That laughter was now replaced with reality.

"We'll probably end up with Grandmother Swain or a foster family because Daddy won't want us."

"No!" Isabella cried, fear making her stomachache worse. She ran out of the house, around the back, and hoisted up the cellar door. Descending down into the darkness, she sat on the cold, damp floor and hugged her knees to her chest, crying.

A few minutes later, Johanna called her name and descended the stairs as well, plopping beside her, out of breath.

"Damn it, Isabella, why do you come down here into this dark hellhole when you're upset? It smells like poop."

"Because it feels safe."

"Oh, good grief," Johanna sighed, putting her arm around Isabella's shoulders. "Look I'm sorry for always saying what I think and scaring you."

"But it's the truth, isn't it?" Isabella asked, sniffing, then lifting the hem of her shirt to wipe her tears off her face. "I'm really scared of that fact. I hate Grandmother Swain so much that I wish she was dead! I do, Johanna! I never wish anyone dead, but I do her."

Johanna was silent for a minute, and then she took a deep breath, exhaled, and hugged Isabella harder. "Listen to me. Yes, it might happen, but I forgot to mention that we have each other, Isabella. We do, right? And I'm not going anywhere. We will always have each other. We always did, and we always will. I love you more than myself, and I'll be with you and you'll be with me. We'll get through anything, and we'll become successful and we'll look back on this time and talk about it while we're sipping champagne."

Isabella smiled a little. Just the thought of them drinking champagne from one of the fancy glasses she'd seen her mother drink from made her giggle.

"We are the best sisters ever," Johanna said, "and I think you know that, don't you? We love each other so much."

"Yes, we are the best sisters ever. I do know that and thank God for you every day." Isabella sniffed again, her tears finally subsiding at the thought of Johanna being with her no matter what terrible situation they faced.

She leaned her head against Johanna's shoulder, and they stayed that way for what seemed an eternity—holding on to each other for comfort in the damp, dark cellar.

The next morning dawned with screaming outside their house.

"Johanna! Wake up!" Isabella shouted, shaking her sister's shoulder as she slept on the couch. "Something is going on outside! There's an ambulance!"

Johanna groggily obliged, opening her eyes and then yawning. When a siren sounded again, she suddenly grew completely alert and then they both ran towards the front door, stepping outside in their nightdresses as the ambulance doors closed.

Their mother was positioned close to the ambulance as Priscilla and Howard wept and hugged each other.

"Oh my God!" Johanna exclaimed to Isabella. "I think it's Grandmother Swain in the ambulance!"

A lightning bolt effect shook Isabella. "It can't be…."

"She's dead! She's dead!" Priscilla shouted, covering her face in her hands and running back into her house. Howard followed, but Juliana walked towards her own house, meeting her daughters on the porch.

"Momma? What happened?" Isabella asked.

"That no-good witch had a massive heart attack last night. Your grandmother is dead."

"It can't be...." Isabella whispered, her voice trailing off as she remembered all too well her wishing her grandmother dead. Guilt, as horrible as she'd ever imagined possible, shot through her until she covered her mouth with her hand and rushed inside the house to the bathroom where she vomited into the newly-installed toilet.

"You better not be getting sick!" her mother shouted after her. "I told you to keep away from sick kids at school. And don't mess up that brand-new toilet or you'll be using the outhouse again!"

The bathroom door opened, and Johanna knelt beside her. "Listen, Izzy," she whispered, reading her thoughts and offering her a wet napkin to wipe her mouth. "Don't you do this. Don't you dare feel one ounce of guilt. You can't take someone's life with words, only God takes a life. Do you understand me?"

Isabella wiped her mouth, then threw the napkin in the trash. Squeezing her eyelids shut, she tried to block out the feelings of guilt. As much as she hated Grandmother Swain and wished her dead, she hadn't known that her wish would come true. She felt like she'd killed her with her bad thoughts. God would surely punish her now.

"Izzy?" Johanna called again. "Look at me."

Reluctantly, Isabella obliged.

"You are not responsible for that evil bitch's death. Say you know that."

Isabella opened her mouth to agree, but somewhere deep inside her lay the fear that she had caused her grandmother's death. She threw her arms around her sister and bawled, not letting up until Johanna pulled slightly apart and smiled at her.

"I hope you feel better now," she told her. "That was a lot of tears, but Isabella, you can't let this play on your gentle mind. You have to toughen up and understand that God is not going to punish you for your thoughts. Grandmother Swain is going to be judged. She was a terrible person to us. You can't help how she made you feel. Don't feel guilty."

"I'll try," Isabella said as Johanna stood and pulled her to her feet. "Let's go for a walk. We're going to miss school, no doubt, because of this, so that's a good thing."

Isabella nodded again, finding it hard to speak as both of them walked back out to the kitchen to find their mother singing a spritely tune and wearing a happy face.

Isabella tried not to remember the next two years. Somewhere as she watched the seasons change, just like an autumn leaf floating on a cool breeze, her and Johanna's lives seemed just as unanchored, just as fragile, and just as uncertain as to where they would end up. The only constants were the instability and cruelty of the people around them.

"One more year after this one and I'll be graduating high school," Johanna had reminded her on the night before the next school year started. The locusts outside their window testified to the closing of summer and the beginning of autumn.

Isabella turned to Johanna in their dimly lit room. Nothing in their environment had changed. They still slept in the living room on a couch. There still was not much food in the kitchen.

But there had been other changes, Isabella thought as she gazed at her sister. Johanna was a complete beauty now. Her frame was slender and tall, her eyes as green as the grass in Ireland they'd seen while looking at scenic calendars. Her temperament, though, had not changed. She constantly disobeyed their mother's demands, and she continued to see the Italian boy she was so fond of, even when her mother was pushing her to date an older boy named Warren.

Isabella had to admit she liked Dominic very much, for he was kind to Johanna and she had not seen that kind of tenderness in any other men in her lifetime. She hoped that her sister would marry him one day, even if their mother objected.

Walking towards the bathroom mirror, Isabella studied her reflection. Johanna had told her that she had blossomed into a beauty as well, but looking at herself now, she wondered if her sister was just being kind.

"You have eyes the color of icy blue," Johanna had told her a few days ago. "Like a light blue sky. And your pale blonde hair and fair skin is what a lot of women in magazines look like now. Don't fret, little Izzy. You are beautiful, and men know that as well, so watch for that idiot next door. I see how Junior looks at you, and it gives me the creeps. He follows you every time you're alone."

Isabella had to admit she was right. And at times, it really bothered her that a terrible thing might happen—like when he tried to get her to take her clothes off.

"Whatcha doin' in there?" Johanna called from the living room, placing a book down as Isabella entered the room again.

"Just thinkin'," Isabella answered, plopping on the couch. "Johanna, I can't wait to be sixteen like you. I wish we were both twins and could graduate school together. I don't want to be here, left without you, when you're gone."

A worried look crossed Johanna's eyes as she stood from the chair and quickly walked over to Isabella. Taking her hands in her own, she smiled. "I'll always be here for you. Maybe not right here in this house, but I'll be keeping an eye on you. We can't ever give in to the bad things people do to us. Life will be kind to us when we leave here. It'll be what we make it, right? We must keep our spirit and mind strong to make our lives great."

"And that takes an education," Isabella added, nodding. She leaned her head against Johanna's shoulder. "And it takes us being there for one another like always."

"That's right," Johanna smiled. "Like always. We'll both go to college."

"I hope so," Isabella said, a feeling in her gut that Johanna wouldn't graduate high school.

And she'd been right.

Junior had seen to that.

A month into the school year, Isabella had decided to walk to a woman's house who had asked her to babysit. Once again she and Johanna had been embarrassed at school for not having enough money to pay for their school workbooks. Isabella wanted to surprise Johanna and find a way to pay for them since their mother wouldn't. They hadn't been able to call their father either since the phone had been disconnected due to non-payment from Juliana.

Isabella started her journey through the woods and down another hill before finding a path to the woman's house.

Suddenly, someone grabbed her from behind, pulling her into the nearby woods. Isabella screamed, and then a hand clamped down on her mouth and one went to her throat. She knew by the disgusting smell of body odor and dirty hands that her attacker was Junior! Lifting her arms, she tried to hit him but he moved and laughed. Then out of nowhere, a huge rock came whizzing by Isabella to strike Junior in the head. He immediately released Isabella and dropped to the ground, unconscious, with blood running down his ear.

Johanna appeared beside him with another heavy rock in her hand ready to strike him.

"No, Johanna," Isabella cautioned, putting her hand out to stop her sister. "That one might kill him if he's not dead already!"

"So what?" Johanna said, kicking him in the side. "That bastard got what he deserved. He was going to rape you, Isabella! What if I hadn't gone to the harbor to pick grapes? I would never have heard you scream!"

"I know, but if he dies, we'll go to prison! Hurry, let's get back home," Isabella pleaded, and Johanna finally agreed as they both ran back in the direction of their house. When they got inside their house, Johanna slammed and locked the kitchen door. Isabella pulled back the curtain to peek out of the window to see if Priscilla was on her way over. Sure enough, she was barreling ahead, furious. "Johanna! She's coming! Where can we hide?"

"I'm not hiding anywhere. Let the witch in, and cover your ears 'cause I'm not holding back, Isabella."

There was a loud banging on the door when Priscilla realized it was locked. She started shouting that the little whore had better unlock the door.

Johanna unlocked the door and jerked it open. "Some nerve you have calling us whores when you're the whore," Johanna said. "I saw you through the window screwing your neighbor when his wife went to the A & P. What are you going to tell your husband about that or your beast of a son who tried to rape my sister, you no-good miserable whore? Does your husband know, like the rest of the town does, that Junior got thrown out of school for trying to molest a little girl? Now, get the hell out of our house and don't come back!"

Isabella didn't think she'd ever seen Priscilla so angry. Her eyes bulged out as she screamed back, "You just wait till your mother and Howard find out about this! She'll beat your asses for days!" And then she stormed out of the house.

Isabella looked over at Johanna with tears in her eyes. "I hope we don't get a beating! I never know if Momma is gonna take our side or not!"

"'Cause she's just as sick in the head," Johanna said, pointing to her temple.

"Take out your history book, Isabella. You have a test tomorrow and you need to study, right?" asked Johanna. "It'll get your mind off of this."

But not studying for a test or anything else could get Isabella's mind off of what just happened or prepare her for what would happen next.

CHAPTER SIXTEEN

"When traveling life's journey, it's good to have a sister's hand to hold on to."

"I am so damn tired of you causing problems, Johanna! Every day I never know what to expect. I don't deserve this shit. You are not going back to school. You're going to get married and get the hell out of this house!"

Those were the words from their mother that Isabella would remember for the rest of her life. Words that had no hope, no beautiful promises, but only the dread of what was to happen to a beautiful life—her beloved Johanna's life.

"This shit?" Johanna repeated. "You're tired of 'this shit?' What shit, Juliana? When's the last time you were hungry and had no food, or had to glue cardboard to fill the holes on your shoes? But damn, look at your pretty nails! Did you just come from getting a manicure?"

Isabella glanced at her mother's nails and noticed that they had been freshly manicured and painted.

"Why you little bitch!" Juliana hissed, moving closer to Johanna. "Your mouth is what gets you into trouble all the time. Well, guess what? All the more reason for you to get married and get the hell out of this house. Someone else can take care of you."

"You're serious?" Johanna shouted back, her face as red in anger as her mother's. "You're going to take their side when Junior almost raped Isabella? I knew you would do something horrific, Juliana, but this surpasses even my wildest predictions."

"That's another thing I can't stand, Johanna!" their mother screamed. "Where the hell do you get off calling me Juliana and not Mom?"

Johanna shrugged, her cheeks still red and her lips blue from biting them. "Maybe I don't because you burned my books or because of the millions of times you've hit me. Or maybe I don't because when you saw that cute guy at the restaurant you told me and Isabella not to call you Mom. After that you never told us to start calling you Mom again so I never did. And you're the worst mother ever, so you're lucky I don't call you what I really want to."

The slap that followed was so loud that Isabella was certain the whole neighborhood could hear it. Johanna took a step forward toward her mother, and Isabella sprinted between the two women. "Please stop this!" she told them, crying and putting her hands out. "Momma, stop it! And Johanna stop talking. Momma, you can't be serious about Johanna marrying! Who could she marry? She's only sixteen!"

Juliana laughed, her eyes narrowing on Johanna's face. "She'll marry Warren, that boy she met at the ice cream stop. He has a job and he's already been telling everyone in town that he wants to marry you. As a matter of fact, I talked to him and his mother about arranging a marriage between you both."

"What?" Johanna cried, shaking her head no, her eyes larger than Isabella had ever seen. "You did that without talking with me? Without asking me what I thought of him? Did you know he's five years older? Did you know I already hate him because he's mean and rude? I'll marry Dominic if I have to marry any boy!"

Juliana laughed, and it sounded as if a thousand demons flew from her mouth. She took a step forward, bending low to bypass Isabella's head and look directly into Johanna's eyes. "Oh, you're not marrying that wop. Trust me on that fact. You're going to marry Warren. And you're going to do it tomorrow before you get crazy notions in your head to run away."

"I won't do it," Johanna snapped, shaking her head. "You're bat-shit crazy! I won't do it!"

But like a clock stopped at someone's death and the black drapes thrown over to cover mirrors, Johanna's life from that moment on became even darker than what was before. Howard had arrived home, and both Juliana and he whisked a panicked Johanna off to Warren's family's house, leaving Isabella weeping and pleading not to take her sister.

Isabella cried for three days when they didn't return. But on the third night, Howard's truck could be heard rolling down the street, and she ran to the front door. But only two of them had returned. Juliana and Howard.

"Where is Johanna?" she cried to them as they entered the front door, searching each of their faces and noticing that her mother's lips were turned upward in a smirk. It was then that she had the answer. Her beloved Johanna was now married to Warren. "Nooooo….." she cried, her voice trailing off as she dropped to the floor.

"Isabella?" a beloved female voice called out, drawing Isabella out of her memories and to the present time. "You trying to lock me out? Come on, Izzy, it's gonna start raining!"

Standing from her rocking chair, Isabella realized she had locked the front screen door.

Placing her teacup down, she hurried to the front door, unlocked the latch, and then threw her arms around her sister's neck.

"Whoa!" her sister laughed, hugging her back. "You really missed me!"

"Oh, I did, Johanna," Isabella told her, leading her into the house. "I really did. I was just thinking about our childhood. I was even talking earlier to a delivery man about us."

Johanna set her purse down on the nearby couch and then turned to her. Isabella was struck, as she often was, with how beautiful her sister was. The years had not faded her beauty, although Johanna's spirit—that never-ending fighter mentality—seemed to have waned some. Isabella hadn't known for certain what had caused the change, but figured Warren, Johanna's husband, was most likely the reason. His reputation proceeded him everywhere he went as a mean trouble-maker, and Isabella had never liked him.

"I try not to remember those horrible times," Johanna said, laughing as she plopped down on the couch, then moaned as if she'd hurt herself.

"What wrong?" Isabella quickly asked, walking towards her.

Johanna avoided her eyes, focusing instead on the teacup Isabella had placed down earlier. "I certainly could use a hot cup of tea. We have all afternoon to catch up, too. Warren is gone for the day, and the kids are all doing their own things. Ever since they reached high school, I hardly see them anymore."

"I'm sure," Isabella smiled, pointing out what a great job Johanna had done in raising them. "I wish I had been around them more while they were growing up."

Johanna huffed. "Well, Warren always tried to keep you away. He knew you didn't like him and was worried you'd talk sense into me into leaving his ass."

Isabella sighed, heading to the kitchen to fill the tea kettle. "He was right. I tried but you were stubborn."

"At least we kept our promises to each other, Izzy," Johanna said, lifting her feet to place them on the ottoman. "We followed through with our education. I'm glad you didn't let a GED stop you from pursuing college. You earned your degree in nursing, and me, well, I absolutely love being a librarian. I'm only working part-time now and taking more college courses at night to work towards my masters."

"We're never too old to learn," Isabella said from the kitchen, smiling as she turned on the stove to place the tea kettle on. "I'm so proud of you."

"I'm proud of you too," Johanna said, and her voice changed to a petal-soft whisper.

Isabella knew that tone well. It was the same loving tone Johanna had used to comfort her when they were children.

After the tea was made and poured, both Isabella and Johanna talked for hours, laughing at old stories and catching up on where everyone was in their family.

"Momma is sick again," Isabella told her. "Did you know that?"

"I try not to stay in contact with her, but I did hear that. I also heard other things as well."

Isabella met Johanna's eyes. "Did our cousin Whitney tell you she thinks Momma is being poisoned by Reynard? Her symptoms are so mysterious that even the doctors are baffled. Whitney also said something about Momma thinking that Reynard and Sergei's wife are having an affair."

Johanna nodded, her face showing a flurry of emotions from curiosity to satisfaction. "I think it's Karma, dear sister, that's come back to bite Juliana in the ass. She divorced Howard to marry Reynard since they'd been having an affair all along, just like I told you back in the day. And now Reynard is having sex with Sergei's wife and they are probably plotting something terrible."

Isabella hoped that Johanna was wrong. "Momma is in the hospital again, Johanna. Maybe we should go see her together and figure out a way to help her?"

Johanna coughed, jerking her cup and sending hot tea over her shirt. "Ouch!" she yelped, standing to lift up her shirt and fan her stomach.

"I'm so sorry!" Isabella exclaimed, knowing that it had most likely been her suggestion that had caused such an accident. "Follow me upstairs to get a new shirt of mine to put on."

Johanna did as Isabella suggested but mumbled under her breath the whole time. "Isabella, I swear no matter how old you get you still seem naïve. Why in the world would I want to help Juliana?" she asked. "Or why would you, for that matter?"

Isabella felt like she was nine years old again and kept silent. Johanna was right. Why should she want to help a person who was supposed to care and love them but had been selfish and cruel? But somewhere inside her were the lessons she'd learned at Miss Aunda's and the church on the hill. And she thought it best to forgive. Maybe one day she could talk to Johanna about forgiveness as well.

She walked towards the closet, pulling out a few shirts she thought Johanna would like and handed them to her. "Take any one you'd like and I'll meet you back downstairs," she told her. "I'll bring out the peanut butter fudge I made from your recipe."

"Sounds delicious. Thank you, Izzy," Johanna said, smiling, and then Isabella closed the door behind her.

Isabella was almost to the stairs when she remembered she wanted to wash Johanna's shirt before it stained. Turning around quickly, she opened the door to her bedroom, then covered her mouth to stifle a scream.

A boot mark, no doubt from a large man's foot, was outlined on Johanna's back at her lower waist. The skin around it was discolored with bruises. Someone had kicked Johanna, and had kicked her brutally. And that someone had to be Warren.

"Izzy! Why'd you come back?" Johanna cried, trying unsuccessfully to cover herself with the shirt, but it was too late. Isabella had seen the abuse.

Isabella rushed to her sister's side as they both collapsed on the edge of the bed.

Isabella burst into tears. "Oh my God, Johanna! Why? Why did this happen? Why are you letting him do this to you?" she asked, grasping her sister's hands. "You're a fighter. The one who stood up to everyone as children! How could you let him abuse you this way? Your skin is marred all over with fresh bruises and old ones. And that horrible boot mark! Dear God—" she couldn't continue but sobbed harder.

Johanna slipped her arms around Isabella. "He's always hurt me this way, but what was I to do with no education at first? I had five babies and was so concerned for them. You know it's only been recently that I could afford to get a degree. But back when the kids were small, there was nothing for me to do but try to make peace with him."

"You could've lived with me!" Isabella told her. "He forced you to start having babies immediately after you were married so you would be too scared to leave him! You had five children by the time you were twenty-three years old! That's insane. And you knew that I said I'd never marry because I wanted to just have peace in my life. I lived alone all these years when you and the kids could've crossed state lines to stay with me."

Johanna shook her head, taking Isabella's hand. "No, sister dear," she told Isabella. "I couldn't have done that. Warren threatened to kill me and the children if I left him. And he meant it. I know he did. He beats me for any reason. Even if the phone line is busy when he calls, he says I'm talking to another man. A few days ago, even his mother saw him grab me by my hair, and she took the broom and started beating him with it to stop him from hurting me further. He told her he'd kill me, the boys, then himself if she dared to tell anyone or if I tried to leave him. I just want to make certain my youngest boys can graduate and leave the house on their own like my girls did. I have to stay."

"Oh, God, Johanna," Isabella said, throwing her arms around her sister's neck and pressing closely into her. "You sound just like an abused spouse. They all say that. That's what those bastard husbands want you to think. That's how they intimidate you into staying. Please, please tell me you'll leave him. Please? Dear God, please say yes."

A few moments of silence ensued. And in that long silence, Isabella knew that the balance of her sister's life depended on her answer. She never prayed so hard for an answer to be yes.

Finally, Johanna drew apart from Isabella to look into her eyes. "Okay, Izzy. I promise if he does one more thing I will divorce him and come live with you until I can afford otherwise."

Letting out the breath she'd been holding, Isabella thanked God and then thanked and encouraged Johanna. "Yes! Oh, my beautiful sister, yes. I'm here for you always."

"And I'm here for you too," Johanna said, her eyes wet with tears. "I might not have much at the moment, but I will do anything for you."

After Johanna left that day, it didn't take long for "one more thing" to happen. Warren, after a tough day at work, arrived home drunk and called for Johanna after he felt the hood of the car and realized it was warm.

Not giving her a chance to defend herself, he'd accused her of visiting a boyfriend while he was at work and the boys were at school, and then punched her in the gut. As she doubled over, he grabbed a sword he kept under the bed. Dragging her by her hair, he'd thrown her in the bathtub, making slicing movements as if he were going to chop her into pieces. She screamed, and the kids who'd just returned from school, ran upstairs to see their father bringing the sword down upon their mother. They jumped on him, knocking him off balance and the sword missed Johanna's head to slice through her forearm.

The police had arrived after being called by the neighbors, and they handcuffed Warren and shoved him into a cruiser. Johanna's arm was bandaged and then she'd packed what she and the kids needed and headed to Isabella's. And true to her word, she set in motion a divorce from Warren. The judge had said it was the worst case of wife abuse he'd ever seen.

"I am so proud of you!" Isabella told her, glancing at the college grades she was achieving. "Soon, you'll be graduating with honors."

"I plan on it," Johanna said, looking around Isabella's house. "Thank you for making this small beautiful house our home too." She hugged Isabella. "We've loved spending these past six months here, but we've got to move out soon. The boys are so disruptive now with their girlfriends, and I feel safer now that Warren married again right outta prison."

"I loved having you all here," Isabella laughed, relishing and thanking God every day for the time she and her sister and nephews spent together. "And my garden has never looked so vibrant. Anything you touch blooms, my dear sister."

"Gardening is one thing that I do love to do with you."

"And you've blessed me with so many gifts for it!" Isabella pointed out. "You not only got my English garden started years ago, but you keep it looking so gorgeous. I especially love the little sitting bench by the pink roses."

Johanna smiled, glancing towards the window where the garden was in full bloom. "I thought it would be perfect there amongst the pink rosebush I planted for me and the white rose bush I planted for you. I just wanted you to have a token of my appreciation for all you've done for me and the boys. My next statue for the garden will be an angel. I believe it was our guardian angels that kept us alive all these years. And I might not have been the most religious person, but I do thank the Lord for you every day. You're the best sister I could've ever hoped for."

"*You're* the best sister, Johanna," Isabella told her, walking towards her to slip an arm through hers as they both gazed toward the vibrant garden. "It's a relief to know you talk to the Lord about anything," she teased. "And I doubly love the fact that it's me you thank him for like I thank him for you." She displayed a hand toward the newly placed garden bench by the roses. "Thank you for that. It's a resting place, and I'll sit there often after you and the boys move out. Whenever I do, I'll think of us."

"We've been through so much here on earth that I think the best resting place will be in Heaven, Izzy," Johanna pointed out. "And I hope God puts our mansions side by side because I couldn't imagine it being Heaven if you weren't beside me." She smiled wistfully, looking off into the distance at the garden both she and Isabella had tended to. "You know, Izzy," she said, her eyes never leaving the flowers in the distance. "Our family was and still is kind of like a garden. One of dark secrets. But the way I see it, good gardeners tend to their gardens like we did this past summer with yours. We pulled out the bad weeds and the diseased plants, and then we watered them and allowed God to do the rest with sunlight. Our lives might not have been the best but we've survived the odds. We didn't let the bad people break us."

"Yes," Isabella agreed, sighing. "We're educated, successful, and on our way to more happiness."

"I guess you can say at this age in our lives, we're in full bloom!" Johanna joked, and they both laughed, hugging each other before the phone rang.

Isabella answered the call, her eyes finding her sister's from across the room. "Yes, how long? Okay, we'll be right there."

"Let me guess. Juliana's taken a turn for the worse?" Johanna asked.

"Yes," Isabella answered, sadness weaving itself around her heart. "It was very sudden. She's been given the last rites. That was Whitney who stopped there to visit with her."

"Juliana's sudden illness is another family secret, no doubt," Johanna said, her expression full of disgust as she walked to the closet to grab two lightweight jackets for both of them, and then scribbled a note of their whereabouts for the boys when they returned home from school.

Within minutes, they were at the hospital but their mother had already passed away.

CHAPTER SEVENTEEN

"Happiness is being with my sister."

The funeral for Juliana hadn't produced many tears from those that should've been grieving the most. Isabella looked at Reynard who stood smiling in the corner of the funeral parlor, his hands casually placed inside his pockets as he bent near to a woman whose stocky back Isabella recognized as Belinda, her cousin Sergei's wife.

"Sister, dear, bend near, so I can whisper my secret in your ear," Johanna whispered after she walked to Isabella's side and leaned in close.

It had been many years since they'd said that phrase to each other, but immediately Johanna's words brought Isabella back to being a little girl.

"Maybe he did poison Juliana," Johanna said low, her green eyes dark as she stared at Reynard. "The doctor told him that it was all metabolic with Juliana. That her diabetes was under control, her heart was fine, but her organs failed. When the hospital told Reynard that Juliana might pass, he responded that it would probably be another "dry run." That's what Whitney told me. She also said that Juliana truly believed he and Sergei's wife were having an affair. That's why they were poisoning her, and that's why Reynard had her body immediately cremated. How ironic. In the end, Juliana got just what she deserved.

She lost her beauty, and no one loved her but you and a few others who pretended she was a better person than she actually was. Even Howard isn't here. And why would he be? She left him for his best friend."

"Please, Johanna," Isabella said, rubbing her temples. "Don't talk about Momma that way, especially since she's gone now. Try to forgive her." She turned to her sister and hugged her. "Please try. As far as her being poisoned, there are too many questions and suspicions lingering, so I agree with Whitney, but what can we do about it now?"

"I don't know, Izzy," Johanna said, shaking her head. "But I have a feeling whatever garden of secrets happened to Juliana is only going to sprout more bad seeds."

"I hope not."

Johanna straightened her back, looping her arm through Isabella's. "Amazing, isn't it?" she said. "Look around, Izzy. What do you see?" Without waiting for an answer, she went on. "Everyone here is all grown up now. Even past middle-age. There's Sergei over there by that giant fern. Handsome as ever and kind-hearted. Poor Aunt Lottie passed away years ago. There's a few of our other cousins in the corner by the window. All from our past as children and all so much older. But nothing has really changed, has it? Maybe for us, it has. We did what we set out to do. We're educated, independent, and healthy. We beat the odds, overcoming what others tried to do to us. But look at them. They're still huddled together, keeping to themselves as if they're holding tight to that garden of secrets I mentioned earlier."

"Good grief, that's depressing, Johanna," Isabella said, not wanting to recognize the truth of her sister's words, but the truth couldn't be denied. Reynard and Belinda were throwing each other stares across the room, while Sergei sat quietly, his hand against his temples as if trying to shut out unpleasant thoughts. Priscilla had actually shown up, but her evil son was not with her. Junior, just like so many people had predicted, was in prison for murder.

As if reading her thoughts, Johanna laughed. "I can't believe that witch had the nerve to show up. It was because of her and Junior that Juliana forced me to marry that piece of shit. I wish Junior had gotten the death penalty. Now that would've been something to watch—with popcorn and Coke-Cola."

"Johanna!" Isabella exclaimed, saying a quick prayer for God to forgive her sister. "Please, stop saying such things at Momma's funeral. Let's go get a cold cup of water. It'll be over soon."

"Not soon enough for me," Johanna said under her breath, following Isabella's lead to the foyer where a pitcher of water and paper cups were set up on a table.

"Hey girls," a feminine voice interrupted as Isabella and Johanna both turned to look at their cousin, Whitney.

"Whitney, how are you?" Isabella asked, giving her a quick hug. "Thank you for all your help in the funeral preparations."

"No thanks necessary," Whitney said, her eyes glistening with tears. "I feel so awful, though, about your mom and what might've happened to her."

"Maybe we should talk about it away from prying eyes and ears," Johanna suggested, throwing a glance towards the crowded room. "You should come by for lunch sometime."

"I would love that," Whitney nodded. "I just have a nagging feeling that more bad things are going to happen in this family."

"Johanna was just saying something similar," Isabella said, not liking the chill running down her spine. For if she was totally honest with herself, she'd agree that something ominous seemed to loom on the horizon.

⁓⁄⁄\⁓

Two weeks later, Isabella set a second piece of chocolate cake in front of Johanna as they sat outside on Isabella's patio, their beloved garden lush with vibrant colors.

"I'm so proud of you," Isabella said, moving her empty plate of chocolate crumbs to the side of the table. Lifting her cup, she took a sip of coffee then set it back down. "You graduated with honors, Johanna! You did it. What a beautiful ceremony this morning. I'm so proud of you."

Johanna grinned, her green eyes sparkling in the bright sunshine. Isabella could tell that her sister felt a sense of accomplishment even though she'd batted down praise all day.

"It's something I had to do," she told Isabella, lifting her fork to cut into her second piece of cake. "We both have now literally achieved what we set out to do, Izzy."

"So what's next?" Isabella laughed, throwing her hands up in the air as if the sky were the limit for their goals.

"Ireland?" Johanna asked, giggling, and Isabella joined in the laughter. Johanna had always wanted to visit Ireland, and maybe, just maybe one day they could visit that beautiful country together.

"I'm up for anything that makes you happy," Isabella said, nodding. "For you certainly deserve some joy in your life."

"We *both* do," Johanna corrected, pointing out that Isabella hadn't had an easy life, either. "I'm so glad you never married, though. Who needs men when we have each other, chocolate, and this beautiful garden?"

"That's right," Isabella agreed, loving Johanna's easy-going manner when she was happy.

They laughed and talked for hours, well into the evening until a knock at the door broke through their conversation.

"Whitney!" Isabella exclaimed, opening the front door to find her cousin peering at her, a dismal look on her face. "Come in. Is something wrong?"

Whitney entered the foyer and greeted Johanna as Isabella shut the door behind her.

"Well, you look like someone just ran over your dog," Johanna said, patting the empty space next to her on the couch. "Come sit. Tell us why you're looking so worried."

Whitney did as Johanna suggested, sitting beside her as Isabella went into the kitchen to make her a cup of tea. When she returned, Whitney and Johanna looked up at her, halting their deep conversation.

"Isabella," Johanna said, pointing to the chair in back of her. "You'd better sit down for this news."

Isabella handed Whitney the teacup, then sat across from them as Johanna stared at her. "Well, go on. Someone tell me what's going on."

Johanna inhaled then exhaled soundly. "Sergei's in the hospital with severe stomach pain and aches that are similar to what Juliana had."

"No!" Isabella exclaimed, covering her mouth. Was Reynard and Belinda now poisoning him as well? "Listen, I hope you both don't think I'm stupid for saying this, but I was watching Sally Jessie Raphael the other morning and there was a woman on who was being poisoned by her husband for two years! The poison affected her legs with pain and she was in a wheelchair, just like Momma had been. He had been poisoning her with arsenic. Maybe we can get the doctors to look at Sergei. What have they said, Whitney?"

"His main doctor who'd looked at him is so damn stupid," Whitney informed, telling them both that the doctor diagnosed him with "Chinese cancer" because he was in the military.

"Who the hell ever heard of Chinese cancer?" Johanna asked. "That's absurd."

"There is no such thing," Whitney answered, filling them in on the details of how Sergei's mysterious symptoms had the medical staff stumped. "Belinda is throwing everything at the doctors and telling them stupid stuff about Sergei being overseas. Every time we suggest something that makes sense, she forbids it from happening. Like wanting to take him to another hospital when obviously this one is clueless as to what is causing his pain."

"Maybe we could see him?" Isabella suggested, looking at them both. "What about now? Can we go visit him? We have to make certain we fight hard for him if there's foul play involved here."

"If?" Johanna repeated. "There *is* foul play. I'm certain of it." Turning to Whitney, she said, "Ask Cole about it, but he told me he saw Belinda and Reynard in a lip lock at the elevators at the hospital where Sergei is! How disgusting is that? Anyhow, maybe we should just sleep on it tonight and see him tomorrow around noon. Isabella and I can meet you at the hospital."

Whitney agreed, wiping her tears with a tissue and then leaving as worried-looking as when she'd arrived.

"Johanna," Isabella called, shaking her head. "We've got to save him somehow. Sergei is such a wonderful person. We can't let Belinda and Reynard hurt him."

"I know, Isabella. I know." Standing up, Johanna lifted her jacket from the back of the couch. "I'll head home now and I'll be back here tomorrow morning to pick you up. We'll try to figure it out as we gather more information."

"Okay, sis," Isabella said, walking with her towards the front door. After closing the door behind Johanna, she leaned against it, feeling as though Sergei wouldn't survive another year.

—⁊⫫—

"What happened to your hair?" Johanna blurted to Sergei as he lay in the hospital bed.

"Johanna!" Isabella called out, motioning for her to be a bit more tactful. Even though she'd just been as surprised to find Sergei completely bald, his trademark of thick grey-brown hair gone, she'd held back from asking in case it was his medicinal treatments that caused the loss.

Sergei shrugged, trying to grin but it fell short and he frowned. "The barber was just here. He shaved it again. He said it would be the last time. It's not growing anymore, and he doubted it ever will again. Belinda wanted me to shave it when I became sick. She's been shaving it for a while now or she hires a barber to do it. She said my hair would mess up the house by falling out if I had to have chemo. I suppose she was right, but I miss it."

"Unbelievable," Johanna muttered.

"Well, you look handsome with or without hair," Isabella pointed out, noticing a small patch of hair by the hospital bed that the barber had missed sweeping up off the floor. She inconspicuously walked to his bed, bent down a second, scooped it up, and put it into her pocket as a memento if his hair never grew back. She'd always envied Sergei's hair. Saddened but trying not to show it, she asked, "Have you eaten, Sergei?"

"Not yet," he answered, shaking his head. "I'm just not hungry these days. How are my kids and grandkids today? Have you seen them? I miss them so much but didn't want them to see me here a lot. It's so depressing, and I want them happy and focused on their schooling and futures."

Isabella sighed, wishing she could cheer him up, for he certainly looked sad, in pain, and extremely thin. "We haven't seen them yet, but we could always stop by your house later today or tomorrow to check on them. And maybe today, we could eat with you. We could go to the cafeteria and bring something back. It'll be like old times, Sergei. Besides, Johanna and I haven't eaten and I'm a bit hungry."

"Hospital food sucks," Johanna said, nodding toward a breakfast tray of some sort of mush in a bowl and burned toast. "Let's not do the cafeteria, Izzy. If Sergei wants something, maybe we can have

Whitney bring him a milkshake and burger today." She smiled at him. "And next time, dear cousin, we'll smuggle you in whatever you want."

"Oh, no worries," he said, and this time he seemed to finally smile fully. "Belinda is bringing me food any minute. She's been doing that every day I've been in the hospital. It's better than that crap on the tray, but today I'm just not hungry."

He had just finished speaking when Belinda entered the room, carrying a lunch box. She stumbled when she noticed Isabella and Johanna in the room, and Isabella quickly reached to steady her.

"Whoa," Johanna said, laughing. "Maybe you wouldn't have been so surprised we were here if you had had told us sooner that Sergei was in the hospital. We could've been visiting him for weeks."

Belinda placed the lunchbox on a nearby end table, unzipped it, and sighed. "It's been so crazy, girls. I'm sorry. Who told you?"

"Whitney," Isabella answered. "She'll be here, too, any second."

"Oh, how fun. A big reunion of sorts, no doubt." Belinda's tone was anything but cordial as she began to take food items out of the lunchbox. "I hope you're hungry, Sergei."

Isabella didn't think Sergei could turn any paler, but he certainly did as his wife moved his leg rather roughly to sit on the edge of the bed with a hamburger propped in her other hand. She offered it to him to take. He turned away. Apparently, the scent of food nauseated him.

"I can't eat," he told her, shaking his head. "Please. I was just telling the girls here I'm not hungry, but hey, Isabella is. Do me a favor and give it to her instead. I'll eat later. I promise."

"Oh, Sergei, no, I can't eat your food—" Isabella began, and was shocked when Belinda cut her off.

"Of course you can't, Isabella," she said, directing a cool stare at her before looking back toward her husband. "It's for you, dear, and you must eat it to keep your strength up," she said, her tone harsh with reprimand.

"Sweetheart," he pleaded, his brown eyes looking ancient for someone only in his early fifties. "I'm sure it's delicious, but give it to Isabella today. I won't be able to hold down one bite and don't want it to go to waste."

Johanna gazed at Isabella, throwing her a "what the hell?" look from the awkwardness taking place. An ornery glint appeared in her green eyes, and then she turned to Belinda and said, "It won't go to waste if you do as your husband asks and give it to Isabella."

Belinda's eyelids, heavily coated with turquoise eyeshadow, raised, and her mouth turned into a grim line. Her hands, which reminded Isabella of her mother's with their freshly manicured nails, trembled—causing the hamburger she was holding to flop awkwardly like a freshly caught fish.

Isabella glanced at Sergei whose eyes were closed as if he had fallen asleep, and then she looked back at Belinda.

"I-ah-" Belinda stuttered, standing suddenly as she lifted the sandwich toward Isabella. But then she dropped it in a matter of seconds and had stepped on it. "Damn! I'm so sorry!" she exclaimed, bending down to retrieve the smashed sandwich stuck to her shoe. "I'm so clumsy!"

Isabella quickly moved to her side, grabbing a napkin from the breakfast tray, but Belinda shooed her away.

"No. I got this mess, Isabella. Don't worry. It's my fault."

Isabella stepped back, placing her hands in the pockets of her jacket as Whitney entered the room and greeted everyone.

"I'm sorry I'm late," she said, looking from one woman to another and then at Sergei who was soundly asleep. "What's going on? More bad news?"

"No," Johanna said first, an expression of disgust on her face. "We were just watching Belinda clean smashed hamburger meat off of her shoe. Sergei's not hungry, and that's a good thing now, considering he's asleep and the sandwich is no longer an option."

"Oh."

Whitney's one word in response summed up all of the awkwardness that had just taken place since Belinda arrived. A short time later, after stilted conversation and more awkwardness, Isabella and Johanna left the hospital.

"What the hell was that all about?" Johanna blurted as they walked toward their car in the parking garage. "She is definitely up to something. Did you see her hands shaking when we were urging her to give you the sandwich to eat? I wish we'd gotten a hold of that sandwich. Maybe we could've had it tested for poison."

Isabella stopped walking, and Johanna paused too, studying her a moment. "What's wrong?"

"I was trying to do that with the napkin," Isabella explained, "but she practically pushed me away."

"Izzy, you're street smart, after all," Johanna said, hugging her. "Maybe next time we can get a hold of something she's trying to force-feed him."

After they'd been seated inside the car with Isabella driving, Johanna turned to her and said, "Let's stop at the library on the way home. I want to do a bit of research on poisons."

Isabella agreed, and a short time later, after they'd seated themselves at a library's table, Isabella looked up from her books and said, "I think it's arsenic, Johanna. I think they poisoned our mother and now Sergei with arsenic."

Isabella went on to explain her reasons with Johanna agreeing, but the final chilling aspect was the shaving of Sergei's hair. "It says here that arsenic is able to be detected in a person's hair. Even one strand will show it under laboratory testing." Disgusted, she pushed the text books away. To think that people could be so evil as to plot, then execute, such a horrific, tortuous act against another. "That's why Belinda was insistent on shaving his hair. There would be no evidence."

"We need to get a hold of a piece of his hair before they shave it again," Johanna said.

Isabella's eyes lit up and she patted the pocket of her jacket and said, "I've got that already, Jo Jo!" Smiling, she told her how she'd picked up some of his hair from the floor.

"Izzy! I am amazed at you! This is great. Now we just need to figure out the next steps."

"But poor Momma," Isabella said, tears welling up. "I didn't do anything for her but rub her legs to ease the pain. At that time, I just didn't know all of this or put the thread together that this is what was happening. At least not until the end when more puzzle pieces were falling into place. I wish I could've done more for her." She knew Johanna would scold her for crying for a mother who was anything but caring and loving, yet for whatever reason, Isabella had loved her in spite of that fact. "She died before she could get tested for poison."

"Well, let's not make that mistake here with our cousin," Johanna said. "Let's go home and then tomorrow we'll talk to Sergei's doctor, maybe even his kids, a lawyer, or something."

But they never got the chance. Sergei was pronounced dead at 3:13 am.

CHAPTER EIGHTEEN

"Because I have a sister I will always have a friend."

"I don't understand this!" Whitney cried into her hands. "Why didn't they just divorce them if they wanted to be together? Why kill them in this torturous way? My poor brother!"

The three women sat in the hospital lobby after just witnessing Sergei's children file out of his room, weeping and holding on to one another for comfort. Belinda was heard yelling at the doctors and staff that they had misdiagnosed Sergei and she'd be suing them.

"But nothing's been proven yet, Whitney," Isabella offered, trying to find some way to console her cousin who had been very close to Sergei. "Maybe we should give Belinda and Reynard the benefit of the doubt."

Even as she said those words, she knew they were ridiculous. Reynard had acted distraught at Juliana's death, but then only a few hours later he'd been seen laughing with Belinda, and then later, kissing her.

Johanna sighed, shaking her head. "You know they did this, Isabella. Deep down, you do. Not only so they could be together, but Belinda gets $125,000 from Sergei's life insurance policy. And Reynard got Juliana's house, car, and what money was left even though he spent most of it beforehand."

"Then what do we do? I'd like to at least tell his doctor our suspicions."

"Maybe we can do that if we see him while we're here," said Whitney.

"Definitely," Isabella agreed, searching the nursing station nearby for Dr. Bradley, Sergei's main physician. He was nowhere in sight.

Sergei had been removed from his room and taken to the morgue. Isabella watched his body leave the room on a stretcher, and memories filled her mind. She remembered playing baseball with him, his quirky grin and the way he'd saved her from Junior many times. She cried softly into her hands as Johanna and Whitney began to cry next to her. Isabella wept for her mother and now Sergei. Even though life had become better for her and Johanna as adults, the pain of so many tragic secrets seemed to follow them everywhere.

When some time had passed, Isabella slipped her arm around Whitney's and Johanna's shoulders. "Sergei wouldn't want us so upset. How about some lunch? We can go back to my house. I have some cold chicken and potato salad left over from yesterday."

Whitney declined due to prior engagements, but Johanna accepted. Isabella was comforted that she'd be spending the day with her sister, for certainly there was too much sadness and unanswered questions about their mother and now Sergei that drained the soul.

Once they arrived back at her house, Isabella and Johanna ate a little more quietly than usual. Gone was the light-hearted banter, teasing, or recollections of the past.

"Izzy, let's go outside and sit by the garden," Johanna suggested. "Everything is so sad right now, and it's a beautiful September day. We should enjoy the weather before winter arrives."

Isabella agreed. They made a pot of tea then made their way outside, teacups in hand, to the patio and lush garden beyond. Sitting on the bench that Johanna had purchased for their special garden, they sipped their tea.

Almost immediately their dispositions brightened.

"Something sort of healing about being surrounded by colorful flowers," Johanna pointed out.

"For sure," Isabella said, and in the distance the phone inside her house could be heard ringing. Leaving Johanna's side, she returned a short time later. "That was Whitney. Belinda is having a service for Sergei tomorrow, then a dinner right after."

"She sure didn't waste much time in getting him buried."

"I know," Isabella said, shaking her head. "Let's go in and watch some TV to get our minds off of this. Maybe by the end of the week, we can talk to Dr. Bradley and see what he thinks."

"That's a good idea."

They both went back into the house with Johanna slipping her arm through Isabella's. "I'm glad we have each other, sister. For surely, this world can be cruel."

"I love you, Johanna," Isabella told her, knowing that her sister was her best friend, confidante, and so much more. She couldn't imagine life without her.

"I love you too, Izzy."

They entered the house, still deep in thought, but with lightened hearts from expressing their sisterly bond of love.

The next day as the hour for Sergei's funeral approached, the phone rang often with Belinda's son, Jonathon, asking if she and Johanna would be attending the dinner after the funeral.

"We are not," Isabella had told him after speaking with Johanna and deciding that they couldn't be around Belinda and Reynard any longer.

"Please come," he urged. "You must. Mother wants you both there."

Johanna had been adamant about not going and Isabella agreed. She turned the invitation down and hung up, but he'd continued to call and leave messages.

"You know what he's doing, don't you?" Johanna had asked. "He's making sure we're going to be there because I'll bet you that Belinda caught wind that we've been talking about her poisoning Sergei and she's going to confront us. I don't want to give her the chance."

Isabella couldn't have agreed more. They both attended the funeral, but it was difficult. Isabella wanted to slap both Reynard and Belinda as they both sat by Sergei's casket with huge smiles on their faces.

After the service at the cemetery where Sergei's burial had taken place, all attendees but Isabella and Johanna went to the dinner afterwards. Staying low key, they hurried away in Isabella's vehicle and headed for home, talking amongst themselves about Reynard and Belinda's cavalier behavior.

Later that night while watching TV to get their minds off of the tragedy of Sergei's death, the phone rang. It was Whitney.

"You're not going to believe this, but guess where Belinda and Reynard are?" she asked them. Without waiting for an answer, she declared through tears, "They went dancing after the funeral dinner, and are having their 'own' private time at the casino!"

Isabella grew nauseous from the news and shared it with Johanna. "So much for the grieving widow."

"There's a special place in hell for people like that," Johanna said, shaking her head. "Poor Sergei."

"And Momma," Isabella added, saddened when her sister rolled her eyes.

"There's more," Whitney told Isabella. "Belinda said that if we keep spreading rumors, she'll sue all of us for defamation of character."

"Let her try!" Johanna shouted when Isabella repeated Whitney's comment. "I'm not afraid of her. I've even contacted Dr. Bradley already and left him a message about our suspicions. He hasn't returned my call yet, but I think we should still pursue justice for Sergei's sake."

"And Momma's," Isabella added, and Johanna rolled her eyes again.

"She plans on suing Dr. Bradley for misdiagnosing Sergei with Chinese cancer. She's already consulted a lawyer. Can you believe it?" Whitney asked.

"But if she poisoned Sergei, why would she draw attention to his death?" Isabella asked.

Johanna heard what Whitney had said and told them her theory. "Belinda is so greedy, and both of them think they can outsmart anyone. She knows Sergei is buried now, and she plans on going after money any way she can."

And true to Johanna's words, the following week, Belinda filed a malpractice lawsuit against Dr. Bradley. Armed with a case that she felt she could win, Belinda incorporated the help of her children, and a meeting was set in place for the first lawyer meeting to begin on Monday.

"Belinda has her family coming to this meeting, even those who live out of state," Isabella told Johanna when her sister stopped by for lunch. "She's made such a big deal of wrongdoing by the hospital and Dr. Bradley. On Sunday, she's going to have a full house, as everyone is spending the night so that they can all go together to the lawyers in the morning."

"This is insane," Johanna said, her green eyes narrowed with apparent disgust as she shook her head as if to dispel the dismal scenario of a brutal murderer winning money for killing someone. "We've got to do something."

After Johanna left that day, Isabella sat and thought of all they'd talked about. How could they help Sergei now? She pondered for what seemed like hours until her eyes lit up and she rushed upstairs, sliding open her closet door and reaching inside for the coat she wore with Johanna when they'd visited Sergei. Reaching into one of the side pockets, she came up empty of Sergei's hair she'd picked up from the hospital floor. Carefully, and with painstaking effort, she gently checked the other pocket, but couldn't find the strands of hair she'd placed inside. "No!" she cried, turning the pocket inside out. Why hadn't she taken better precautions not to lose his hair? It could've fallen out, undetected by her, as she and Johanna walked to their car that fateful day. And now they'd never be able to have it tested for arsenic.

Hauling out shoes and her clothing, she searched the carpet in and around the closet, but nothing. Defeated, she collapsed against the wall and cried.

—/ı\—

"Oh, my God! What happened? Are you serious?" Isabella exclaimed a few days later as Johanna called her on the phone. "That would be the best thing to happen, especially since I lost the lock of his hair! How did this come about?"

"Apparently, after learning that Belinda is filing a malpractice lawsuit, Dr. Bradley must've taken our suspicious seriously and told his lawyer to fight the malpractice suit by setting in motion a court order to exhume Sergei's body for autopsy!"

"That'll prove he was poisoned for sure," Isabella said, thankful that justice would be forthcoming, for she felt in every bone of her body that he had been slowly murdered along with her mother.

After the phone call with her sister, the weekdays to the initial lawyer meeting seemed excruciatingly long for Isabella. She'd heard all kinds of rumors during that time, but the most interesting was how Belinda had handled the news of Sergei's body being exhumed.

She was rumored to have screamed and thrown a lamp against the wall. "They want to exhume his body! No! There is no way I'll let that

171

happen to poor Sergei. We will not exhume his body. I'd rather drop the lawsuit."

Isabella had learned about Belinda's reaction after speaking to Sergei's daughter whom she'd bumped into after running an errand.

"But we are going to pursue it even if Mom backs out," she had told Isabella. "We know she's under too much stress and is grieving so we're going to pursue it for her. We're still meeting at her house this Sunday night to travel to the lawyers on Monday morning."

Isabella had shared this new information with Johanna, but no sooner had Monday arrived than new developments flooded the family.

Johanna banged on her front porch door Monday afternoon.

"What's going on?" Isabella had asked, hurrying to unlock the storm door as Johanna barreled in and plopped down on the sofa.

"You're not going to believe this," Johanna said, her eyes moving to the ceiling as if she, herself, was still absorbing whatever she'd be telling Isabella next.

"Go on!" Isabella said, sitting next to her. "What is it? What happened?"

Johanna shook her head slowly then turned to Isabella. "Sergei's family couldn't make it to the lawyer's office today to file the malpractice suit. Whitney called me shortly ago."

"They couldn't or decided not to?" Isabella cried, exasperated and curious as to what was going on. "Sister, dear! Tell me! Ugh!"

Johanna grabbed Isabella's hands and looked her straight in the eyes. "They spent the night at Belinda's. Belinda kept telling them she did not want them to pursue the case because it would be sacrilegious to have Sergei's body exhumed and he would not want that."

"And?"

Johanna continued shaking her head as if in disbelief. "They were still going to pursue it against Belinda's wishes. She made them dinner and they went to sleep. In the middle of the night, everyone, and I mean every one of them, including Belinda's eighteen-month-old grandchild, came down with an intestinal virus and flu-like symptoms. They were vomiting and running to the bathroom."

"Oh my God! That's horrible!"

Johanna nodded, clicking her tongue. "Yup. And being as naïve as they are, when Belinda told them that it was a sign that God and Sergei did not want them to pursue legal action, they believed her and decided to drop the lawsuit."

"I'm trying to wrap my mind around this," Isabella said, envisioning the scene of so many sick at one time. "And none of them questioned that she had cooked for them and that she, herself, didn't get sick?"

"Nope. Not one," Johanna answered, leaning her head against the back of the couch. "Her children totally believe in her. Like she's practically a saint. Their spouses are probably suspicious, but who knows?"

Isabella sighed, trying to digest all that Johanna had just told her. "How in the world are we going to come to terms with this, Johanna? We both know that Momma and Sergei were poisoned by Reynard and Belinda because of their affair and their greed. So how do we live with that knowledge? It's going to eat me up."

For a long time, both of them just sat there. No music on. No TV. Both of them deep in their own thoughts until Johanna finally said, "I think I know, Isabella, and you do too. We've got to believe that Sergei wouldn't have wanted his children and grandchildren to know that he'd been poisoned by their mother. He would've wanted them to live healthy productive lives without the stigma of their mother being a murderer."

"Yeah, but—" Isabella began then stopped and gathered her thoughts. Perhaps Johanna was right, but what if they began poisoning others? She shared her concerns with Johanna.

"It's unlikely she'll harm her kids. You know how she's always doted on them," Johanna said. "But we are stuck here. Without proof, I think you and I aren't going to be able to do anything. She'll fight anyone to keep Sergei's body buried. I'm sure she was upset Sergei's wishes were against cremation because no doubt she'd have done that to his body."

"So we let them get away with two murders?"

"My sweet sister, now where's your faith?" Johanna smiled, pointing out that Isabella had always been the one to rely on God for revenge. "You used to tell me that God would take care of Junior and that an evil person will never go unpunished. Now Junior's in prison and his son was killed by stealing copper from someone's electrical wiring in their home. I think that Belinda and Reynard got what they wanted, and now they'll either turn on each other, or something later in life will happen to them. Whether God, Karma or something else, justice will no doubt follow their evil doings. So let's take a deep breath, exhale, and move on, knowing that's what Sergei would've wanted. Like I said earlier, he would not want his children to live with the stigma of their mother being a murderer. He'd rather sacrifice the truth for their well-being."

As much as Isabella wanted to see justice served immediately against Belinda and Reynard, she had to admit that what her sister said made better sense.

"Then we do nothing and let God be God, huh?"

"Exactly," Johanna answered, her voice turning soft and reminding Isabella of when she'd console her after Grandmother Swain had beaten her.

Isabella let out a deep breath, reaching for her sister's hand and squeezing it. As long as she had Johanna by her side, she would be strong and let God be God to watch over them both.

CHAPTER NINETEEN

"Sisters are different flowers from the same garden."

The next four years went by more calmly than any years previously. Isabella sat outside in the garden, waiting for her sister to arrive. Since Sergei's death, their usual routine had been to meet at least twice a week to take in every precious moment of a calmer life and the sisterly affection that they shared.

"Sometimes when I look back on the tragic years," Johanna told her later as they clipped roses and tended to the garden's soil, "I think of how much beauty was still able to come from so much pain."

"What a lovely thought," Isabella said, leaning back on the mat she'd placed for their knees as they bent low to the ground. She studied her sister for a moment. Even in her mid-sixties, Johanna's beauty hadn't dimmed with the passage of time. Her eyes were still a fiery green, her auburn hair still thick and soft, and her skin, even with a few creases and fine lines, appeared youthful. "I like how quiet these past years have been. It's like we've been able to breathe after so much pain and loss in our lives. Momma is gone. So is Daddy, Howard, Aunt Lottie, Sergei...."

"The only one of those people I miss is Sergei."

"Oh, Johanna," Isabella smirked, rolling her eyes. "Will you ever stop talking ill of the dead?"

"Probably not," she laughed, leaning back on her behind to take off her gardening gloves and place them on the walkway.

Isabella continued studying her, noticing that her eyes seemed more reflective today, as if she was in deeper thought than usual.

"I am happier than I've ever been, dear Izzy."

"Well, I'm glad about that," Isabella told her, wondering what had her sister in such a contemplative state. "You're single, attractive, with an empty nest, and you have your dream job as a librarian and a master's degree…. what's not to be happy about?"

"It's all good, true," Johanna said, tilting her head to steady her gaze on Isabella. "Still, there are times I awake in fear at night, and I think we're back at Juliana's and Howard's."

"They're gone now. No one can hurt you like that any longer."

Johanna's eyes glistened with tears. "No, Izzy," she said. "It's not that I'm scared they'll hurt me, but you again. What Grandmother Swain and that wretched Ann Bailey did to you, and then Junior almost raping you, well, I know I put on a tough exterior at the time, but I was always riddled with so much anxiety about how to protect you when I had no weapons but my wits to do so. I was even scared when you'd be around Belinda and Reynard without me there, but I put on a brave face. I still hope they get what they deserve for murdering Juliana and Sergei. And even now, years later, I still worry about you, and I'm not sure why. You're settled with a successful business, yet I will always feel the need to protect you. Isn't that crazy?"

Moved to tears by her sister's tender words, Isabella shook her head. "Of course it's not crazy. You were thrust into a terrible situation being the oldest. But you're tough as nails, Johanna. You were a force to be reckoned with then, and you are now. I can still envision you lighting into Junior like a windmill that day he followed me into the woods."

Johanna laughed, nudging Isabella's shoulder. "Maybe then, but the passing of time has a way of mellowing even the toughest people. Every day I think about our lives, fighting for survival, having so little.

Every time I buy a new pair of shoes, I think about the ones we wore to school with cardboard taped over the holes."

"I think of that every time I put on my shoes," Isabella said, hating the fact that so much had happened in their lives that they'd be forced to remember those bad memories for the remainder. "I remember how I was forbidden to wash my hair so that I'd get teased at school. I remember running from Junior and how Grandmother Swain would lie about me so I'd get punished. And many times, I still miss Aunda, Annie and Rags."

"I wonder what ever happened to Miss Aunda."

Isabella smiled. "Me too. Momma told me she had died, but I wonder if that was true."

"Probably not," Johanna said, shrugging. "Maybe we should try to find her someday."

"I'd like that."

"You know, that time period, and of course our relationship, were the only happy times of our childhood. I couldn't imagine, Izzy, if we didn't have each other."

"We won't ever have to worry about that now," Isabella pointed out. "We'll grow old together and sit on rocking chairs while griping about the price of food."

Johanna laughed, nudging her again with her shoulder. "I'll probably still be cursing like a drunken sailor, and you'll be prim and proper as always. We certainly have beaten the odds, though, haven't we? In today's world, there's so much more to help protect abused children. We didn't have any of those outreaches, but somehow, we did what we set out to do and became educated and successful."

"I think the human spirit can endure a lot as long as the mind stays positive and focused."

"And hopeful," Johanna added. "Which is something you always were, my sister. I know I teased you a lot for being so naïve, but I always admired your faith and your ability to forgive."

Isabella's eyes filled with tears. She knew how much her sister loved her, but she'd never known that she actually admired some of the traits she'd teased her about. Slipping her arm around Johanna's shoulders, she couldn't find her voice until the tears subsided. "Thank you, and know that I always admired you. We balanced each other out then, and we still do now."

"I agree," Johanna nodded, turning to look at the lush garden in full bloom. "This is a beautiful garden, isn't it? There are still so many secrets buried in family lineage." Her eyes lit up and she said, "Oh that reminds me! I saw Edwin at the doctor's the other day. Every time I look at him, I wonder if he's our brother and not a cousin, you know? But that's another secret that might not be revealed in our lifetime. Just like seeing Belinda and Reynard come to justice. Although hearing that Junior got what he deserved and died in prison gave me new hope that we'll see vengeance happen to Reynard and Belinda soon."

"Things will come full circle eventually," Isabella said, standing slowly and then offering her hand to help Johanna to her feet. "How about we go inside and order pizza? But first, what were you doing at the doctor's office? Were you getting your mammogram results from the exam on your birthday last month? Is everything okay?"

Johanna stood, brushed the dirt from her jeans, and then shrugged. "Well, I didn't make it to the mammogram exam," she admitted, and then after seeing the disapproving look in her sister's eyes, defended, "Don't start nagging, Isabella. I have an appointment next month. We had plans on my birthday, remember? And I didn't want to have an exam break up our day. That's why I went to the doctor's office, so that I could reschedule, and that's when I ran into Edwin. He's got a bad cold."

"Poor Edwin. He was always sickly. Well, how about I come with you next month to your appointment and we can go to lunch afterward, then do some shopping at that new mall that opened near Robinson?"

"Sounds good to me!" Johanna laughed as they gathered their gardening tools and headed inside. "That's exactly what I'd like to do after getting my boobs smashed."

"Sounds like the perfect therapy to me."

"Well, then, let's do it," Johanna agreed, placing the pail and spade she was holding on the porch. "But I know you're wanting to go with me to make certain that I go this time. However, I will tell you that I would go no matter if you were there or not. My left breast has been so sore since I fell a few months ago."

"You mean when you locked yourself out of your house and climbed onto the kitchen roof to try and get inside the window?"

"Yup," Johanna smirked, her green eyes lighting with laughter.

"What a stupid thing for me to do," Johanna grumbled, heading inside the house as Isabella held the door open for her then followed. "First I lock myself out, and then I try to climb onto the roof. I almost made it, though, but slipped at the last second, took a nasty fall, and landed on my breasts, of all things. And the breast that had that lump I was telling you about! Wow, did that hurt! It still does."

"Then it's a very good thing you're finally doing what the doctor suggested and getting a mammogram."

"I guess so," Johanna shrugged, washing her hands under the kitchen faucet, drying them, and then walking towards the sofa to plop down. "I don't have much faith in hospitals or doctors, but I'm glad you're in the nursing field. The hospitals need more caring staff like you and your employees. Now, let's order that pizza. I'm starved."

Isabella washed her hands, then picked up the phone and dialed the local pizzeria. She couldn't wait for a relaxing night watching TV with her sister, so she put all thoughts of mammograms, their childhood, and the future behind her. This night was about having food in their stomachs, money to maintain a comfortable lifestyle, and thankfulness, as always, that they had each other.

—✒—

"Isabella," Johanna called to her two months later as she arrived on her doorstep.

"What is it?" Isabella asked, ushering her in and not liking the worried expression on her sister's face.

"The doctor called me about the results of my mammogram and he wants to set up an appointment to talk to me."

"He didn't give you any other information?"

Johanna shook her head. "No. He wants to talk in person."

Isabella grew faint, putting her arm out to brace herself against the arm of the sofa. She couldn't let Johanna see how concerned she was.

"Hurry, let's both sit down," she said, trying to smile. "So he wants to see you. That happens all the time. He might want to go over that nasty fall you took. Maybe you hurt yourself more than we thought."

"Maybe," Johanna agreed, her eyes lowering to Isabella's hands. "You're wringing your hands like you used to as a little girl. Good grief. That's not good."

Isabella separated her hands, then sat on them on the couch, laughing. "I am not that worried. I just don't want you to be. Let's find out what's going on and not borrow trouble for things we don't know for certain. Okay?"

"Okay."

"Today is really early yet and the doctor's office might have cancellations. How 'bout we call the doctor back and see if you can get in today. I'll go with you, of course. There's no sense in having our thoughts scatter all over the place when we can nip it now and find out what's going on."

"I agree, Izzy," Johanna said, shaking her head. "It'll be tortuous to wait longer. If it's bad news, I want it now. If it's not so bad, I want it now, too. I never liked being kept in the dark about things."

Isabella glanced at the phone. "Give them a call. Let's do this together."

A few hours later, after receiving a return call that the doctor could speak with Johanna but at the hospital office where he was on call, Isabella drove them to the hospital and tried to keep the mood light by discussing everything else but the appointment before them.

Once at the hospital, Johanna walked up to the receptionist and asked where Dr. Sterling's office was. The receptionist looked at her notes in front of her, found Johanna's name, and then pointed down the hall. "The oncology department is located at the end of the hall and to the right. Room 112."

Isabella's knees weakened, a foreboding sense smothering her. Nauseous, she inhaled sharply. *The oncology department...the oncology department....*

Not a good sign, she thought, close to tears but not wanting Johanna to see them as her sister filled out the necessary forms. Johanna placed the pen down on the last form, then turned to Isabella, her eyes dulled but a smile playing around her mouth. Isabella knew that look. One of fear yet strength. She'd seen that smile on her sister many times during their childhood.

"Izzy," she whispered, giving a sharp movement with her head toward the hall. "Ready?"

Isabella straightened her spine. Her sister needed her strength now and she'd be damned if she was going to fall apart. The fear of the unknown was worse than knowing. She'd be strong for Johanna no matter what.

Once seated in Dr. Sterling's office, he stepped into the room a few minutes later, closed the door behind him, and sat across from them at his desk. "Hello, ladies," he said, his paperwork and folders on

Johanna's results in partial view. He then sighed, took off his glasses, and tapped them softly on the desk.

The wait for him to speak was excruciating.

"Doctor, please," Johanna said, her voice sounding strong. "Talk to me."

He lifted his head, stared straight into Johanna's eyes and said, "The results of your mammogram show that you are in stage four of breast cancer. My theory is that the lump you had been feeling in your left breast had grown considerably, and was already cancerous, obviously. However, when that breast took the brunt of your fall, the lump was punctured so to speak, instantly spreading the cancer to all other areas. I am so sorry."

Silence filled the room, and Isabella could only think of how sometimes silence is the most deafening sound of all.

With her head spinning, she fought the temptation to pass out. *Not Johanna. This couldn't be. Not her beloved sister. She couldn't be dying....*

She felt Johanna's hand on hers and a squeeze.

"Is there treatment available?" Johanna asked Dr. Sterling.

He shook his head, his expression grave. "There is, of course, but this cancer is aggressive and in the latest stage. It's unlikely that treatment now will help you, but there is the possibility it can prolong your life and give you more time."

It was those words... his factual tone threaded with the experience of medical science that sent Isabella into a panic. Standing, the room darkened as if she were falling into a black hole.

"Are you all right?" Dr. Sterling asked her.

She could hear his question but it seemed to come from somewhere off in the distance. She couldn't answer him. And then she was falling, backwards, deeper into an abyss of blackness.

"Isabella!" Johanna cried somewhere close in the abyss. "Hurry, sit down. Sit down!"

Someone pushed her down, and she landed solidly, hearing voices telling her to breathe.

She obeyed and soon the room came into focus and she saw the worried expressions of her sister and Dr. Sterling. Her sister was looking at her as if she wanted to help ease the pain that this tragic news brought to Isabella when it was Johanna who was the victim.

Embarrassed and appalled that she'd almost fainted, Isabella apologized.

"Don't apologize, Izzy," Johanna said, her eyes spilling over with tears. "It's okay. Just breathe. We'll get through this together."

"I should be comforting you," Isabella said, "and instead, I'm acting selfish and I almost passed out."

"It's a shock, ladies," Dr. Sterling interjected, looking at both of them. "No apologies are necessary. Shock affects everyone differently." He leaned back into his chair, looked down at Johanna's medical chart, then back up at her. "Do you think you may want treatment? If you do, we must start it immediately, like tomorrow."

"And it may help to give me more time?"

"It may, but the treatments will be just as aggressive as the cancer. You must be prepared for that."

"Do it, Johanna," Isabella said, wanting as much time with her sister as possible. If there was the slightest chance her sister could be cured, she wanted it.

Johanna deliberated, asking more questions until agreeing.

"Then your first radiation treatment will be tomorrow at 7 a.m. here at this hospital. Just go to the front desk and they'll escort you and get all the preliminaries taken care of."

When they left the hospital that day, Isabella had never felt more like a robot. Her movements were slow as if she'd forgotten how to walk naturally but was doing it by memory. Her heart was breaking, and that was the only sign that showed she was alive. For surely, she had died with the news that Dr. Sterling had given them.

The year that followed was just as brutal as that fateful day. Her beloved sister had gone through sixteen radiation treatments and several rounds of chemotherapy. Gone was her beautiful trademark auburn hair, and instead, she now wore wigs, a few of which had garnered the only laughs they'd experienced as Johanna tried them on.

Johanna's pallor had also changed considerably, and even though the side-effects of the treatment were expected, there was a brutality to watching a loved one wither away slowly and to lose half her body weight, her hair, her strength. Yet in her sister's eyes, she could still find that bright spark to survive.

One particular difficult day as Johanna struggled to walk, Isabella, who'd been caring for her ever since her first treatment, studied her intently. "Jo Jo," she whispered, "lie down. I'll turn on a soap opera for you. You can romanticize about those hot men on there."

Johanna smiled, doing as Isabella suggested and lying down slowly, moaning as her hips, which were now so fragile, made contact with the cushion. Immediately, Isabella lifted a softer pillow that had fallen on the floor and propped it as comfortably as possible under her sister's legs.

When Johanna had fallen asleep, Isabella sat across from her like she usually did now and rocked on the chair opposite her. She watched over her like a mother hen protecting its young. For minutes that seemed like hours, she deliberated about all that had been and all that was present with her sister's care. And then she stood and went upstairs to use the phone in her bedroom.

"It's Isabella, Dr. Sterling," she greeted, thankful that he'd answered her call. "I'd like to ask you what your true opinion is on my sister's timeframe. How long will I have her in my life, Dr. Sterling? What do you think, since you've watched over her care and treatments?"

Dead silence ensued again. The kind that was deafening.

"The reason I'm asking, Doctor, is because my sister has always had a lifelong dream to visit Ireland. I'd like to make that dream a reality for her. But I want her to be in a better physical state to enjoy it. We would be gone for about two weeks."

"So you're asking me to postpone chemo?" he asked. "And if I think doing so won't make a harmful impact on prolonging her life?"

"Yes."

More silence, and then he said, "I can hold off giving Johanna chemo treatments because she is in the last stages of her cancer and there are no more medicines available to help her. With or without treatment, I don't see her being with us past four months."

Isabella covered her mouth, but the sorrowful wail had already burst forth.

"I'm sorry," he said, his voice grave. "But by all means, Isabella, take your sister to Ireland. Go! Have a wonderful time. Let her experience all that Irish splendor and the love you two sisters share." His voice cracked with emotion. "I must tell you that it's been something to witness. The love and bond you both have has been an inspiration to everyone here at this hospital, including me. I want Johanna to be set free, so to speak. She's fought the good fight. And you've fought alongside her, but now it's time for her to fly. Go to Ireland. Love life together while you can."

"Thank you, Doctor. Thank you," Isabella said through the tears that wouldn't stop flowing. She hung up the phone, went into the bathroom and covered her face with a towel to muffle her sobs so as not to wake her sister, and then she wept as if she'd already lost her. When she'd emptied herself like a well running dry, she straightened, splashed cold water on her face, and stared in the mirror at her reflection. "It's time, Isabella," she told herself, summoning up strength to face the future and make it the absolute best for Johanna. "It's time for Johanna to smile."

—⁊⁊⟨⟨—

Johanna stirred awake, her movements slow and painful until her eyes opened and she found Isabella near. "Hey, sis," Johanna whispered. "I'm sorry I slept so long."

"No apologies. You need your rest."

"I should be getting up and dressed for my next treatment."

Isabella shook her head. "Nope. Not now. Let's go outside to our secret garden. For certainly it's been a place, just like our phrase we say to one another, where we share our secrets."

A half hour later, Isabella supported Johanna as they stepped out to their garden where the sun warmed their faces and beautiful roses in bloom surrounded them like nature's very own floral canvas.

"This sun, fresh air, and scent of roses feels so good," Johanna whispered, breathing hard from her walk outside.

"It does, doesn't it?" Isabella asked, helping her sister take a seat on the bench. "Our secret garden, and I have a secret to share."

Johanna's eyes lifted. "You do? What are you up to now, Izzy?"

"Oh, no. I can't tell you yet until I say...*Sister, dear, bend near, so I can whisper my secret in your ear.*"

Johanna leaned in.

"Where have you always wanted to visit if you could go anywhere in the world?"

Johanna sighed. "That's a question, not a secret, and you know where, Isabella. Ireland. A land that I'll only visit in my dreams."

"Are you ready for this, Johanna?"

"Ready for what?"

"We are going to Ireland, dear sister. That's my secret. It's already been taken care of while you were sleeping. We leave in two weeks. And during that time, there will be no more treatments so you'll be at your best to enjoy your dream come true."

"Are you serious? You really mean this? We're going to Ireland? No more treatments?"

"You betcha."

Johanna started crying, placing her head in her hands. And then she lifted her face to look at Isabella and there it was—a smile so big it reached from east to west.

Bullseye, Isabella thought, thankful she'd accomplished what she'd set out to do for her sister. The sun was setting, and Isabella was reminded that just like the closing of a day by night, her sister's time on earth was closing as well. Swallowing hard, she dismissed such grim thoughts and smiled back at her. "I know you're tired, Johanna, but you'll start to feel better by then, and it's a ten-hour flight to Ireland so you can have all that time to rest on the plane."

Johanna practically squealed in delight. "Thank you so much for surprising me with this trip, Isabella."

"Don't thank me. We would do anything for each other. You'd do the same for me."

They sat in the garden a while longer and discussed the trip's itinerary, and two weeks later, they landed in Ireland and taxied to their hotel room. There on the couch, Johanna slept for a long time and more peacefully than she had in a year.

When she awoke, she realized that they'd missed a complimentary dinner downstairs in the hotel.

"Oh, Isabella, why didn't you wake me? It's now 9 o'clock. We'll never get dinner and I'm starving."

"I wasn't going to wake you when you were sleeping so soundly. Besides, Johanna, we might be in a different country but certainly every country has "room service" in their hotels."

Isabella found a food menu underneath the room's phone.

"Now *this* is what I call living the dream!" Johanna exclaimed after they'd picked their food items and called in their orders. "We never would've dreamed of being able to do something like this while we were kids. Ireland, room service, and now the fact that the little hair I have left on my head might start to grow again are things to celebrate tonight, Izzy!"

Isabella turned her back quickly. She couldn't let Johanna see her cry, but thoughts of not having her sister for long filled her. When she turned back to Johanna, she smiled and Johanna walked over and hugged her.

The hug which was meant to be a joyous act shocked Isabella. She could feel every one of Johanna's ribs. Why such a fact shocked her now, she didn't know because she'd helped her dress many times.

Room service arrived a short time later, and then as if God, himself, had said there would be no more sadness for a while, their adventure truly began. Whether laughing at the Irish dialect and amazing people they'd encountered, to things as simple as watching the emerald-green landscape glisten with morning dew, both of them became enchanted with the country that was their temporary "heaven on earth."

On their last day before they left for the airport and home, both decided that one more gaze at the ocean atop the cliffs needed to happen.

Their driver, who'd been hired as their chauffer and guide during the two weeks, took them to his special place which he felt was the most beautiful spot in the country. There, standing on the highest peak, they overlooked the ocean in all its splendor and dreamlike landscape of sea, cliffs, and vibrant colors as deep as Johanna's eyes. Both stood in silence while the strong winds refreshed them and the sun bathed them in delight.

"Maybe this is what Heaven will be like, Izzy," Johanna whispered. "And maybe we'll have our mansions right next to each other."

Isabella closed her eyes tightly and nodded.

It was a long, meaningful moment, along with the whole trip, that would be carved into their hearts forever.

"Ladies," the driver called to them, his Irish lilt a pleasure to Isabella's ears. "We must be goin' if we want to see you pretty ladies home to America."

And they agreed, each deep in thought as they eased inside the car. Reaching for each other's hands, they held on tightly as the car preceded to an unknown future, leaving Ireland behind them but taking its wondrous memories with them.

CHAPTER TWENTY

"Sisters are special, from young ones to old. God gave me a sister.
More precious than gold."

"We've been back home now, Isabella, for a week. I should call Dr. Sterling and see if he wants me to continue treatments."

"I don't think that'll be the case," Isabella told her, remembering her last conversation with the doctor.

However, regardless of what had been discussed during that phone call, Isabella found herself driving Johanna to his office to discuss her future treatments.

"Thank you for always driving me," Johanna told her inside the car. "Even though it's a short distance, I just get so tired behind the wheel these days."

"Johanna, you know I don't mind. I will always take you. I am here for you. Always."

They arrived at Dr. Sterling's office earlier than usual. He seemed the same as always, somewhat dismal and frustrated that he was put in a position to be the bearer of bad news.

"Good morning, ladies. Did you enjoy your trip to Ireland?"

"Indeed!" Johanna exclaimed as they sat down in their usual seats by his desk. "Did you know, Dr. Sterling, that it was my lifelong dream to see Ireland?"

"I think a little birdie told me that," he smiled, glancing at Isabella. "I'm so happy you both enjoyed yourselves. That's the best medicine ever."

"Speaking of medicine, do you want me to continue treatments?"

Dr. Sterling cleared his throat, and looked away then back at Johanna. "No, my dear," he said, rubbing his temples. "No. You have been a brave soul and fought hard until now, but there is nothing more I, nor medical science, can do for you. We've exhausted all options. It's all in God's hands now."

Johanna accepted the news calmly, and thanked him for his time and care. When they stepped outside his office, Isabella reached for her hand and she grasped it as they walked silently down the hall, outside the building, and to their car.

It wasn't long after leaving his office that day that Johanna's condition worsened. Plagued with pain, hospice was soon dispatched and the decision made that a nursing station be set up in Johanna's own house instead of Isabella's due to an easier layout for mobility.

"There you are, little Izzy," Johanna told her one day as Isabella arrived at her house. "My kids just left and now I've been waiting for you."

"You have?" Isabella smiled, placing a plate of spaghetti on the end table. "But I'm usually here all day long and at the usual time with your food. Today I made you my famous spaghetti. Do you think you can eat a few bites?"

Johanna closed her eyes a minute then reopened them. "Thank you so much for the food every day, but today I'm just not hungry. I've been wanting to tell you something."

Isabella touched Johanna's hand softly. "What is it, Jo?"

"Oh, no," Johanna said with a grin that tilted the corners of her mouth. "First things first. Let me begin by saying….*Sister, dear, bend near, so I can whisper my secret in your ear.*"

Isabella leaned in.

"An angel appeared to me," Johanna whispered. "And did you know that angels don't have wings, Isabella? Not the ones closest to God. They are wingless and so beautiful. And the angel said to me that God sent him to tell me that I will dwell in a mansion just like the ones we talked about. That God has prepared a special place for me. Isn't that wonderful? And little Izzy, I know that my mansion will be next to yours one day. I just know it. Thank you for all you've done for me and all the love you've given me throughout our lives."

"Johanna, please," Isabella said, crying softly. "God has made us sisters, and love has made us friends. What a wonderful blessing we both have had."

A knock on the door sounded, and Isabella could see from the living room window that the hospice nurse had arrived to administer more pain medication to Johanna.

Minutes later, as Johanna settled more comfortably on her bed, she looked at Isabella. "I'm tired now and you look a mess," she said, grinning. "Why don't you go home, take a shower after I fall asleep, and work on that pile of unopened mail that's probably on your table? I worry about you, dear sister."

Isabella nodded. "If that's what makes you happy, I'll do that, but only after you've fallen asleep."

"Deal."

Isabella held Johanna's hand, and Johanna signaled that she wanted to bring Isabella's hand closer to her mouth. Isabella helped her by lifting it, and Johanna kissed the top of it saying, "No matter what happens, we'll be together again in our heavenly mansions side by side. Remember that, dear sister, and remember how much I love you. I will always be with you just like when we were children."

"I love you too, Johanna, and I will remember. I promise." Isabella let the tears flow freely, and she waited until Johanna had fallen into a comfortable sleep before she left her in the care of Rita, the compassionate nurse who'd been assigned to Johanna's case.

A short time later, after she was home and showered, she stepped out of the bathroom and the phone rang.

An electrical shock shot through her.

She rushed to the phone and answered it, but she already knew in her spirit that her beloved sister had gone home to be with Jesus. She hung the phone up after Rita confirmed the tragic news, and then dropped to her knees, shaking uncontrollably.

She would never again see her sister's face again or the deep twinkle in her eyes.

"God, please!" she cried, her voice breaking and sounding hollow as blackness suffocated her. "How can I live without her? We shared one heart, and now mine is only half..."

Burying her head into her hands, she wept.

━╱╲━

The garden was in bright colorful blooms when months later, Isabella visited it and sat on the bench Johanna had given her. This garden was her sanctuary—the place she still met her sister each day in her thoughts, heart, and memories.

The sound of a loud truck in front of her house signaled that Frank, the FedEx driver, had arrived. Minutes later, he came around the corner of the house holding a large box. "Where would you like this, Miss Isabella?"

"Right beside me is fine," she answered, smiling as he placed it beside her and she began to open it. "It's a garden statue. I've been adding little details to my and Johanna's garden each day."

"I'm so sorry about your loss. She seemed like a mighty fine person like you. She was strong."

"She was, indeed. She was a giver, too, and even donated her body to West Virginia University for research."

"That's an admirable act."

She talked with Frank a bit longer, and after he left, she took out the statue from the box and positioned it near the rose bush in Johanna's honor. Wind chimes sweetly tinkled in the distance, and it was almost as if Johanna was showing her approval for the new statue through the timely melody.

Isabella smiled. She loved when God sent her these unexpected moments of comfort. It was during these unexpected occurrences that she envisioned him winking at her and reminding her that Johanna was with him now, happy and free of pain.

Isabella thought of the instant she'd felt Johanna's passing. She'd been told by Rita that the "electrical shock" she'd felt was most likely Johanna's spirit passing through her body on her journey to Heaven, and giving her a last goodbye since they'd been so close.

"I miss you, my beloved sister," Isabella whispered aloud. "I'll never forget our past or how we overcame so much. You're a part of me and always will be."

She thought of how their two lives had intertwined as one during their childhood and then through the rest of their lives as adults.

Looking around at the garden lush with a variety of flowers, she watched two butterflies chase each other playfully, then land on a vibrant pink rose.

Just like how we used to play with each other, Isabella thought, recalling happier times at Miss Aunda's. "But how do I continue living each day without you for the rest of my life? God, how can I do this?"

The breeze stilled, the birds seemed to stop chirping for a moment, and then a calm settled over Isabella's heart and she remembered. Smiling through tears, she breathed deeply, taking it all in, the sights around her, the scents of nature, and the memories that had been planted within her from a lifetime of a garden of secrets.

And then, she exhaled them all, knowing what Johanna would want, remembering what Johanna had asked of her, and determining that she would live her life exactly that way. The way her sister would've wanted.

With faith that they'll see each other again one day.

But she also knew that her heartache would only end permanently when God brought her home to live in the mansion right next to Johanna's.

"My grief will always be present," she whispered, "but I'll remember what you said to me that last day, and how much you loved me, Johanna, and that you'll be waiting for me in our mansions when that beautiful angel, closest to God and without wings, carries me home to you."

Standing, Isabella brushed the soil from her pants and wiped her tears with her sleeve.

Glancing at the garden statue one more time before heading inside her home, she studied it long and hard and then smiled. A true, genuine smile that reached her broken soul.

The statue was in the form of an angel, perfectly placed and ever watchful over two young girls as they frolicked in a beautiful garden— a sisters' garden of secrets.

⸱⸱⸱

ACKNOWLEDGMENT

The completion of this book had been a long, loving journey inspired by the devotion of my sister, the support of my husband and children, and the editorial wisdom of Karina Garrison. With a grateful heart, I thank them all.

In Forever Bloom

The weeds covered the site where a brilliant garden once flourished.
I walked along the parched earth, missing you, my sister,
as I brushed against thorns and rocks. Each step was a memory.
Each pause a whisper to Heaven.
Could you hear me?
Why did you go away?
My feet stumbled on uneven ground, the soil hard and unforgiving
as I caught myself against it. Tears fell to the spot I crumbled at,
watering seeds of doubt to sprout into unflinching certainty.

For there it was, one perfect flower, your favorite rose
standing proudly amongst tangled brush.
Resilient, beautiful,
each tender petal a beacon of your undying love
reminding me that you still lived...
in my memories,
in my heart,
and now in Heaven
where we'll meet again.

For you, my sister, are in forever bloom,
like the rose I now touched
and the garden we once tended,
our love comforts me here
until the day I am beside you,
caring for our garden together,
in that spectacular place
that forever blooms.

~K. Garrison

Thank you for reading *Sisters' Garden of Secrets*.

For new releases, upcoming events, or to contact Pearl Preston,
please visit her website:
www.pearlsofinspiration.com

Made in the USA
Monee, IL
09 May 2020